TIME OUT OF MIND

Klaus and Lynda Schmidt, and the Shahzada,
Prince of Chitral, in the garden of his palace
Photo Frank Fitzgerald

TIME OUT OF MIND

Trekking the Hindu Kush

by
Lynda W. Schmidt

Library of Congress Catalog Card Number 79-90967
Published by Thea Wheelright, TBW Books, Woolwich, Maine 04579
ISBN 0931474-11-6
Composition by Pine Tree Phototypesetting
Manufactured in the USA by Halliday Lithograph, No.Quincy, Mass.
First Edition

CONTENTS

LIST OF ILLUSTRATIONS

Scene from top of Thui An Pass

I

The idea first came to us in Russia, six years earlier. We were then on a wild two-week east to west and back again air tour of that diverse country. Heading west from Khabarovsk in far eastern Russia, through the cold-in-August endless forests of Siberia, to the powder-dry desert of Central Asia, we stopped, suddenly awed, in Tashkent. Here we were in Sidney Greenstreet country, with sinister restaurants and slow-turning ceiling fans. Enormous Oriental looking men with single pigtails hanging down their backs sat at the tables. We drank vodka and champagne in huge quantities, ate and danced to international music.

But the main thing that held us was the extraordinary mountain range to the south. Rising thousands of feet straight up out of the desert, the peaks loomed over us with their snow tops and jagged sides. Some were twenty-five thousand feet high and more, according to Alexei, our guide. These were the Pamirs.

We decided that we would go there on foot one day. But the idea faded away into a back corner, and we went, instead, to other places. We went by boat all around the Mediterranean. We went to investigate, and possibly purchase, a delicate 15th-century-cum Roman watchtower castle, extruded vertically from the top of a pinnacle just outside a small town in northern Italy. We went to East Africa to look at animals and geological formations. Again we went to the Mediterranean to see Beirut in the last month before its destruction, and to Israel, especially Jerusalem. There we felt we were at the beginning of the world, and this image reactivated our earlier thought of searching out the wild back-reaches of the Himalayas.

1

Surely, the Himalayas were as much the beginning of the world as Jerusalem and the Oldavai Gorge.

Somehow we received a schedule of mountain trips from a Colorado friend much given to treks in Nepal. The people who put these mountain trips together were just across the bay from where we lived in San Francisco, and we talked of going to see them. But we did not.

Christmas of that year, 1975, we made a three-day train trip from Vancouver to Montreal. The first part wound through the Canadian Rockies, stark and lovely snow peaks and mountains, and the Himalayas came into our thoughts again. In Montreal we went to the movies, "The Man Who Would Be King," set in what purported to be Kaffiristan, the western Himalayas of northern Pakistan. Now at last it came clear, and we decided. On our return to San Francisco we contacted the mountain trip agency, and signed up for a three-week trek in the Hindu Raj and the Hindu Kush ranges of the western Himalayas. Immediately to the north of these ranges lay the Pamirs. It was classified as a "C" trip, which meant you were assumed to be an experienced hiker and backpacker. We were neither.

Altitudes, once in the Himalayas, would vary between seven and sixteen thousand feet, and only part of the trek had been scouted by one man from the agency. We would go in the monsoon season, and there was reason to believe we would be delayed by flooded valleys and washed-out bridges. Or worse: we were asked to sign a waiver of responsibility for our physical safety.

There was something murky in our approach to the trip. While we were careful with our travel arrangements and our accumulation of recommended equipment, something stayed in the shadows.

We did not prepare physically for the trek. Except for short weekend walks, we did nothing special. Neither of us had hiked for more than a day at a time, or carried a backpack for over twenty-five years. Our office lives and city diet kept us soft and a bit heavy. Alcohol and mattresses were very much part of our daily life. Once we drove up Pike's Peak, fourteen thousand feet, but only to stand and wonder and watch our fingernails turn blue. That was also twenty-five years before.

2

Trekking the Hindu Kush

We planned a few days in India before the trek. We stayed in Old Delhi, explored the city, drove the extraordinary three-hour trip to Acra to see the Taj Mahal. We ate the sometimes difficult food, watched the sometimes difficult street scenes. Then, on my forty-fifth birthday, we flew to Lahore, in Pakistan, to stay a few more days. The monsoon rains began, and there were twelve inches of rain in twenty-four hours. Everything—roads, animals, people, houses—was soaked and submerged. Deaths. No place for the water to run off to. It just stood, and everything stood in it, or drowned.

The lights went off in our hotel on the first day of the rains, and stayed off. But we had an enormous suite of rooms, the only accommodations available, according to the desk clerk, with six rooms, two of which were full bathrooms. We could use only a small space at a time, however, the space illuminated by the few candles available. The water stood a foot deep on the hotel lawns and reflected back whatever candle or other light passed by.

An elegant wedding took place in the middle of all this. Everyone dressed in handsome materials and brilliant colors.

Between storms we caught a flight north to Rawalpindi, Siamese twin city to Islamabad, the capital of Pakistan. Rawalpindi was the jumping off place to the western Himalayas, and it was here that we were to gather with the others of our group. This included two leaders from the mountain travel agency, sixteen clients, and any persons who were to be hired locally.

II

In Rawalpindi we arrived at our hotel, the Kashmir Wallah, and our uneasiness began. It was not a matter of the modesty of the establishment. The Hotel Oberoi Maidens in Old Delhi, and Faletti's in Lahore were not that much more comfortable, for all that they were known as "Grand Hotels." Even being told that our six-room suite at Faletti's number 55, was the one preferred by the Aga Khan when he visited Lahore did not make the comfort greater, or the lizards fewer.

Our uneasiness began in front of the Kashmir Wallah when our driver demanded a thirty per cent higher fare than we had agreed upon at the airport. His aggressive attitude was provocative and it became a matter of pride for both him and us to stick to our guns. A number of people began to stand around and gawk at us, and we felt strongly our foreign-ness.

I went to the front door of the hotel to get someone from inside to arbitrate. The doorman was a dwarf, no more than three feet tall, wearing a tall white hat like a cook's. Reaching up to the door handle, he pulled it open for me. The hotel desk clerk came out at my request and, in brisk Urdu, discouraged the driver from further argument. We paid; he left and we went into the hotel. The front door was again held open by the dwarf.

The clerk denied knowledge of others of our mountain group, though we had been told to register at this hotel by the trip agency. Our unease deepened. What were we doing here, at the end of the world, anyway? Our children and friends had questioned us repeatedly as to our reasons for a trek into unexplored regions of the

5

Himalayas, and we had not really answered them satisfactorily. Because we did not know yet ourselves.

Now, here we were in a small town in northern Pakistan that we had never heard of before this time, and as far as we could tell, we were without countrymen or language. We did not speak Urdu.

We put our belongings down in our room. It had, unaccountably, two square pillars from ceiling to floor right in the middle of it. Perhaps they were holding the ceiling up. The space remaining was small, and by the time we had arranged suitcases, duffle-bags and ice axes, we had almost no floor space left, so we climbed on the bed to consider our next move.

Reviewing the information sheets mailed to us before we left San Francisco, we found a list of names of our co-trekkers. Also a note that a second hotel, Flashman's, was a possibility if the Kashmir Wallah was full.

After an embarrassing series of wrong dialings, I did finally get through to Flashman's Hotel, and to our leader Jock, who had for some reason elected to establish us all there instead of at the Kashmir Wallah, as we had been directed originally.

We went at once to the second hotel to meet Jock and were not comforted. He was the blowhard, attention-demanding, misanthropic variety. People had a function, namely, to listen to his stories, mostly doom-laden, and otherwise to keep out of his way. We went to dinner with him, and our spirits sank as we listened to him hold forth. He had returned a few days earlier from a trip to another area of the mountains, and was full of horror tales about the dangers and delays, the monsoons and terrible rigors encountered. He repeatedly warned us of the hard times we would face, and indicated that once in the mountains we should not expect to come out for a long time.

We are both professional people with definite commitments to others, and we said as much. We played right into his hands thereby. The extra week we had allowed for monsoon delays, as requested by the trip agency, was not enough, according to Jock. He seemed to feel that the only way to arrange for our prospective trek was to have no return commitments. We made a mild effort to explain that we would not have been able to afford the trip at all if we had as cavalier an attitude toward our professions as he suggested. He did not hear us. His hearing, in fact, was impressively nonfunctional.

We tried to find out what plans he had for getting started on the trek. Not much had been done as yet. We would have to wait several days in Rawalpindi. There were papers to be negotiated with the police, since it was entirely against governmental routine for a foreign group to go into the Himalayas where we wanted to go.

Then there were the supplies, which were to have been shipped in barrels from California: no sign of them yet in Rawalpindi.

Local people had to be hired on: one from the army to legitimatize our trip, another from a local trek agency as assistant to Jock. Both these men were indispensable for language (not only Urdu, because in the farther valleys there were numerous variations of language); for negotiation with porters and donkey owners; for familiarity with the type of terrain we would be covering, though they, too, had never been where we were going.

All these plans seemed reasonable, and we had no difficulty with the facts. The attitude, on the other hand, was another nudge to our unease.

Jock kept a parallel commentary running alongside his description of the plans. This commentary had to do with the likelihood that the two Pakistanis, Jahangir and his assistant Saïd, would be unable to reach Rawalpindi because of the rains and floods. That the supplies from California would probably be lost en route, since Pakistan International Airlines could not be counted on. That—and this became a constant refrain for the next few days—the weather would not permit a flight into Gilgit, the first stop in the Himalayas. That flights could go only at six-thirty in the morning, because the weather always collapsed after that, and only two flights at most would take off per day.

And finally he said, "Ins'allah!" Meaning, "God willing." And said it, and said it.

In deepening anxiety and foreboding, we settled down to wait for the beginning of our trip.

7

III

That was on Monday, the second of August. Tuesday and Wednesday the rest of our group turned up, a number of them having flown from the U. S. to Rawalpindi together. Only one duffle-bag was lost en route, belonging to a man named Tom, and it was relatively easy to replace its contents through pooling surplus gear from the rest of the group. There were no outfitting shops for treks in Rawalpindi, since there were no treks going into this area of the Himalayas. In fact, as we came into Rawalpindi, the customs officials scratched out the word "trek" and substituted the word "expedition" on our entrance papers. A trek is a trip over a reasonably well-known and travelled route, while an expedition is a trip through new terrain. Trekking is unknown as yet in northern Pakistan, though common enough in the Nepalese Himalayas. We were the first group planning to walk through these areas. In the last two years, there had been one mountain climbing group from Switzerland and another from Japan, each attempting to conquer a peak in the region. The Japanese had successfully climbed theirs; the Swiss had failed. Our route was to pass the peak that had defeated the Swiss.

Tom's duffle being lost did result in one serious problem. His boots had been in that particular bag. Next in importance to good health are one's boots, comfortably worn-in, for an extended trip on foot. Tom tried to get the airlines to track down his duffle-bag, but we were now in the Middle East, and since the prevailing attitude was the eternal "Ins'allah," he got little help. At any rate, God was apparently not willing, because the duffle did not show up. Jock gave Tom a new pair of boots that he had been planning to break in

9

gradually. Dubiously, Tom accepted them, realizing full well that he was in for trouble with his feet.

As for plans for getting started on our trip, however, nothing seemed to be happening. Of the leaders, only Jock and Ray, his assistant, were present. The Pakistanis were still delayed by the monsoon floods. The barrels of supplies from California had not appeared either. The palavers with local officials went on and on. It was really doubtful whether we would be allowed to go at all.

My husband Klaus and I had a private dilemma, too. In the first place, Jock's continued storytelling of the demands of our trip began to undermine our already shaky confidence. In the second place, by Thursday we began to worry about our return date. In order to be back in San Francisco by August 30, we would have to return to Rawalpindi by August 28. The minimum number of days of actual walking was planned at eighteen. Another minimum of three days was required to fly out of the mountains, since a backlog of passengers was always waiting for plane seats. Finally, given floods and washed-out bridges and trails, we should figure a couple more days.

By these computations we were already pushing our luck. We made an arbitrary decision: If we did not fly out of Rawalpindi into Gilgit by Friday, August 6, we would leave the expedition. If the group left Friday, we would be allowing twenty-two days, which was cutting it much too fine. But having flown fifteen thousand miles to get here, and knowing we would never muster courage enough to try again, we were ready to risk this much.

The days from Monday to Thursday in Rawalpindi had passed slowly. The climate was difficult, to say the least, with great heat and thick humidity. A general lassitude set in, laced through with anxiety. Clearly we were going to be heading into something beyond our experience, and we did not know if we could do it. Yet, once committed to the expedition, there would be no turning back or leaving the group. One was not allowed to travel anywhere in these mountains without a representative from the Pakistan army. Prison was a likely possibility if you were found unattended. One could imagine the prisons.

Jock's attitude unnerved us further. He had little enthusiasm for babysitting anyone. If you were prepared to figure things out for yourself, then you would be allowed along. He took no responsibility, although as titular head of the trip, he expected a certain respect from us all. Luckily for us, his assistant Ray was of another style altogether. He was an extremely reserved man, but had a quiet warmth about him that was very reassuring. Unlike Jock, who was new to leading a group, Ray had been doing this work for several years and seemed not to mind our presence too much.

By Thursday we had explored the town and neighboring sights completely. The local restaurant was quite satisfactory, but eating there day after day rather exhausted its novelty. I discovered one drink, however, that I found to be a great comfort. Called "salt Lassi," it was similar to buttermilk, which I do not like at all. Perhaps it was the situation that made the difference; at any rate, I consumed endless numbers of these tall, cool, salty milk drinks.

Then suddenly, Thursday afternoon, things began to move. Papers were signed, the Pakistanis arrived, the barrels of supplies materialized, and we were galvanized into action.

Jock told us that we would leave for the airport at five the next morning to catch the six-thirty flight into Gilgit, but not to expect it to work out since the weather was unpredictable, and many other passengers were in line ahead of us for seats. Furthermore, we should repack our duffle-bags with as little gear as possible; anything over twenty-five pounds per person we would have to carry on our backs. Also, he said, if we wanted to leave messages to be cabled home in the event we did not return to Rawalpindi by August 28, a local agency claimed to be willing to do that. Of course, he could not *promise* that they would, but at least there was nothing to lose. There would be no communication with the outer world once we got into the mountains.

We composed a telegram saying, "Delayed by monsoons," to be held by the agency until August 28, then sent if we failed to turn up. It was an unsatisfactory arrangement at best, since the wire would not indicate when we would be back, nor even whether we

11

were still alive. Still, taking a number of deep breaths, we proceeded to repack and prepare for departure—Ins'allah—the next morning.

Up at four o'clock in the morning and all the excitement of departure. It was quite dark still, and that heightened the nervous agitation among us. Talking and giggling, we hauled our gear out to the waiting vehicles that were to take us to the airport. Jammed together in too-few spaces, surrounded by duffles and barrels of supplies, we groaned and joked in vain efforts to relieve anxiety.

At the airport, what seemed to be hundreds of people were waiting for the one plane, a Fokker with forty seats, to load and take off. The weather was unstable, clouds coming and going. In the direction of the mountains, too far away to be seen, the weather was somewhat cloudy, and Jock told us triumphantly that we probably would not get to go today, just as he had warned. In fact, he said, we might have to make numerous false starts like this. Since there were no instrumented flight techniques, the pilots had to rely on reasonable visibility to find their way.

One member of our group, Charles—at age fifteen he was the youngest—began to indicate nausea. With the pitch of anxiety all around, it was not surprising; possibly he was expressing something for us all.

After a long wait (actually about one and a half hours), it was decided that our group of twenty would fly. In vast relief, now that there was action to be taken, we surged on board the two-engine plane. There was a release of energy, of expectancy, of thrill from us all, as we jockeyed for seats. High-pitched chatter, laughter, and enthusiasm rose as we began to believe that we were actually going.

And we went. As the plane climbed out of the airport, rising above the flooded flatlands extending in all directions from Rawalpindi, we craned and squinted into the distance to discover the mountains.

Finally they began: rank upon rank of dry, rock-strewn slopes, crisscrossed with tracks into and out of narrow slits of valleys. Here and there pitiful bits of green surrounded what seemed to be isolated huts or sometimes several huts huddled together.

"Do you think we'll have to walk on tracks like that?" someone asked.

"Oh no," someone else said, with a laugh. Then, after a pause, "At least, I hope not."

The ranks of ridges began to change into more peaklike formations, though still in rows, one behind the next. Snow began to appear high up on these increasingly jagged formations. Now the plane began to fly among the mountains, rather than over them. It had reached its ceiling of about twenty thousand feet, and the surrounding peaks were now reaching heights of twenty-five thousand feet and more. Those with their cameras out began to move around the plane, feverishly trying to capture each new sight.

Then a mountain came into view so huge as to dwarf the others. This was Nanga Parbat, nearly twenty-seven thousand feet high, with massive sloping shoulders undulating down from its great peak. We were flying below its top, and we had to crane to look up at it. I felt a sickening lurch in my stomach; this mountain was too big to assimilate, and I turned away from it.

Nanga Parbat saw thirty climbers killed before someone got to its top. And here we were, presuming to enter such country ourselves. Unskilled, middle-aged, new to high altitudes, what were we expecting of ourselves and the Himalayas?

As we came sliding down the erratic air currents into the narrow canyon that was the Gilgit airport, we looked at each other. The flight had been heady and exhilarating at first, but now we felt chastened and awed. What was it going to be like?

The Jeep road between Gilgit and Yasin

IV

Gilgit is a timeless town of the crossroads variety. Here the local people come for supplies and socializing. It is also a place where cultures meet, sometimes in curiosity, sometimes in collision.

For us it was many things, the stop in Gilgit. As we climbed down from the plane, we entered what I felt to be a "timewarp" or psychic slippage. The difference in the atmosphere the staring people, the old-fashioned plane, the elegant Pakistan International Airlines crew, the creaking carts for luggage, the miniscule donkeys, the peculiar pajama-like outfits on the local residents, all were disturbing. More disturbing than the strangeness of Rawalpindi had been.

Perhaps having been brought up to seven thousand feet contributed something to our disorientation. It was as if we were standing on Donner Summit, only to find that we were at the foot of all the mountains.

Gilgit lies at the bottom of a valley. Its sides are sheer inclines up to razor ridges thousands of feet above. The inclines are rubbled rock, with erosion cutting its rills in vertical stripes. Slate-colored and bleak, these rough new formations seemed poised above us, ominous, and liable to crash down.

It was August and warm in the thin air, perhaps eighty degrees. With the monsoons washing away the snow and glacier packs, the rivers were active, and the peaks mostly bald. However, one extraordinary, distant peak was still glacier-covered.

Gradually, I noticed more, and my disquiet increased. Western modes mingled with the strangeness of eerie terrain, alien-looking people, donkeys. The floor of the valley had been cultivated;

good use had been made of its rich earth, deposited by the flooding river. Corn was growing amid apricot trees, and cows and chickens were about. Motor vehicles bearing some resemblance to jeeps scooted around us. Yet the Western touches were just strange enough to be doubly strange. The women were curious about us, but ducked behind their veils. The men were impassive as they scrutinized us. We were intruders.

As our duffle-bags were piled together, we checked to make sure we had them all. One was missing, and most of our supplies did not arrive. They were not expected before tomorrow morning's flight, which was all right, because we needed a day in which to make arrangements for the next stage of the trip.

Young Charles, who was sick on the plane, was lying flat and nauseated in the grass alongside the landing strip. He was ringed around by his parents and others, and finally brought to his feet. We were loaded onto jeeps with our baggage and taken to the town "Rest House." This was a pleasant, government-run establishment in the English style, with lawns and gardens and rooms that looked onto them, each with its porch. It all looked Western, but again, it wasn't.

We had a room with two high beds and a bathroom adjoining. A thin blanket was on each bare mattress and a thermos of water was on the table. The bathroom had a shower head suspended in the middle of the room and, incredibly, a flush toilet.

That evening, as we came back from our shy investigations of the bazaar, the electricity went out. With that, all semblance of Western style ended. The water stopped running because there was no electricity to operate the pump; the tiny lamps went dark. The staff of the Rest House swung into what was obviously a standard routine of candles, buckets of water to wash in and flush the toilet with, warm bottles of beer. We had seen the last of electricity, or anything else of familiarity for the duration.

The next day Charles was feeling better, but his older sister, Karen, had become sick. As it turned out, she had the opportunity to remain in bed, for our supplies did not come with the morning flight and we were delayed another day anyway. Since there was no

16

guarantee that the stuff would be delivered soon, if at all, we began to worry again about ever getting on our way.

Jock continued his doom stories; Karen got sicker; we walked again three or four miles into the bazaar to look at the shops. At this stage of things, I did not know what to make of the items up for sale. Everything was dirty or broken or fly-covered. Shoes were made of plastic; woollen things were discolored and full of stickers. Cheap cloth was hanging torn and dusty. Tea was being sold and drunk by the cupful, but was unappetizing, with street dust settling on its milky surface. Unidentifiable bits of meat or chicken were being cooked, again coated in dust and swarming with flies.

It took a long time to recognize that the goods and cooking belonged to the setting, and as a result inevitably incorporated additives from the air, irrigation ditches, and the soil. But by then our attitude toward dirt had been dramatically revised.

Finally, to appease the growing restlessness of the group, Jock arranged a short local trip to explore the Hunza Valley extending from Gilgit north toward China.

In its capacity as a crossroads town, Gilgit had provided us Americans with a polar opposite group to react to, namely a number of Chinese engineers. As we walked gingerly among the noisy, gaping shopkeepers and customers of the bazaar, we were jolted periodically by the sight of jeeps filled with fierce-looking Chinese. Their car doors and windows tightly closed, they would speed through the littered main street, scattering livestock in all directions. Suddenly, one jeep would turn down an alley, the others following closely behind. As they disappeared they left us with an image of Oriental expression analogous to the ambivalent smile of the Cheshire Cat. Apparently, they did not know what to make of us either. We were not able to clarify our impressions of the Chinese because we never actually met them. Yet we felt the collision of our oppositeness.

So when Jock suggested a jeep trip up the Hunza Valley we were intrigued. We would have a chance to see the great highway the Chinese were putting through the Himalayas from the Chinese border all the way south to Islamabad. No one knew just what this road was

17

for, but apparently it was to be a modern day trade route. We discussed the possible political implications of this great passageway through previously impenetrable mountains.

The Chinese forbade foreigners from examining or approaching their road building, now nearing Gilgit, but the western side of the river was open to us. From there we could look across at the straight line of their construction. The road we were on was a startling contrast. It snaked in and out of ravines, crawled across cliff faces, dropped briskly to the river's edge, then shot straight up again. Six of us were jammed together in each small jeep, and we clung on for dear life as the driver was forced to shift gears over and over again. The surface we were driving over was as perilous as the route itself. Great chuckholes, washed-out places, fallen rock, massive overhanging boulders that were so low we had to duck. Perhaps most frightening of all were the artificially created sections of road. On some of the cliff faces, the builders had been unable to chip into the cliff, so they had built in thin air. They would balance a couple of rocks, stick little twigs between the rocks, lay a piece of wood across, more little sticks and rocks, grafting the whole thing together bit by bit. Finally they would bring in dirt to make a driving surface. I decided the whole system must be sustained by faith, because there was not enough engineering to account for it. The drivers were convinced apparently that Allah was content, because they sailed over this track at maximum speed—which varied from one to twenty miles per hour. Whatever the speed, it was always too fast for the conditions.

From our horror-filled road we looked with increasing envy across the Hunza River to the Chinese road, flat and wide and straight. Big earth-moving vehicles, trucks, and workers were busy on it. In this valley, running north and south, the heat rose during the day to over one hundred degrees. Yet the workers toiled long days there, on tours of six months at a time. The Pakistani attitude of casualness toward this effort impressed us. In this part of the world, we realized, one works all the time.

After a couple of hours of this river scene, our road turned abruptly west and we began climbing steeply up a narrow canyon,

18

still in constant peril and fear. At the farthest reaches of this canyon, after perhaps another two hours of driving, we arrived at an alpine scene totally at odds with the spare, dusty, rock-strewn mountains we had been travelling in. Although we were at about nine thousand feet, the cliffs opened out into gently rising slopes, with ski lifts and chalets. The whole scene was as shocking as if we had never seen a ski area before, simply because of its incongruous location. In a country where all is work and grim survival, here were the playthings of the leisure class.

Yet as we began to "see" better and better, we realized that in fact the grimness of the Himalayas was leavened in many ways. One of the homeliest of these was the custom among the men of the Hunza Valley of picking a fresh flower for their caps. Only then did I realize that there were indeed flowers in the area, tough, colorful, utterly outnumbered by circumstances, yet ubiquitous.

As we ate in the near dark of insufficient candles at the Rest House that evening, then stumbled around with a flashlight to get ready for bed, we compared notes on the effects of the day's trip. Respect for the people of the Himalayas, awe of their mountains, uncertainty of our capacity to endure the coming march, and a general body discomfort were the main reactions.

My ankles were quite swollen, and I worried about edema. Terrible tales of pulmonary edema stuck in my memory; was this swelling in the ankles a warning?

In Gilgit we began to use iodine crystals to purify the water, and we had some anxiety about the effect of iodine on our bodies. Our health seemed good, but the fact that Charles and now Karen were sick made us realize how vulnerable we all were.

As for the increasing buildup of dirt, well, Klaus and I had both been dirty children, and we were not particularly bothered by that. Although the dust churned up by the jeeps was miserable and there would be nothing to do about matted hair and gritty teeth, we were far less worried about dirt than personal safety and stamina.

How to prevent a heart attack from fear of the jeep roads was not clear, however. And our next stage was to be a ten-hour drive into the mountains over ninety miles of just such roads.

At dinner that evening it was decided that we would begin this next stage first thing in the morning. The rest of the supplies and luggage had arrived, jeeps and drivers had been hired, formalities concluded. Tomorrow we would make our commitment to the Himalayas.

V

By eight o'clock the next morning, we had eaten breakfast and piled up our gear on the front verandah of the Rest House. We sat or stood around, watching the loading of the jeeps. Jock was pontificating; Ray was sorting supplies. He checked off containers of freeze-dried food, each with its pretty label: Butterscotch Pudding, Beef and Potatoes, Diced Carrots, Eggs, Macaroni and Cheese. Tea, powdered milk, sugar. Cans of cheese and sardines. "Atta," the local flour; I never did find out what grain it was made from. Cooking equipment such as primus stoves, kerosene, utensils; also tarps against monsoon rains; medicine, several light tents.

The heap of baggage grew. Provisions and equipment for three weeks for twenty people, plus porters and donkeys. I was unnerved to realize that the four jeeps parked in front of this mountain of gear were all the jeeps we would have. Somehow, not only baggage but twenty people and four jeep drivers would have to fit into four small jeeps and travel the ten hours in one day to our next stop, deep in the mountains.

This next camp was a village named Yasin, at the far end of the negotiable jeep road. We were in luck here, because the recent heavy rains and floods had not taken out any of this road. Once the road is washed out there are delays of weeks or months before repairs are completed.

With the baggage mountain complete, loading could begin. Much shouting and commotion ensued, packing and unpacking, trying this way and that to sandwich all the duffles, camera bags, ice

21

axes, food and equipment into the too-small spaces. Yet after a couple of hours it was done. The heavily loaded jeeps stood ready.

Now we twenty-four had to load ourselves on. It is called travelling "Hunza style," to ride perched lightly on top of full loads of luggage. Secretly I did not believe it possible. Surely there were more jeeps coming and we were being teased about the situation.

Yet, inexorably, the loading of passengers proceeded. The driver and two others sat in front, the middle person jammed against the gear shift and interfering alarmingly with its manipulation. In the rear, perilously balanced above the center of gravity, three more clung to roll-over bars, trying not to think of them as roll-over bars.

Klaus and I sat in the rear, feeling magnanimous in letting others up front, not realizing the disadvantages they would endure. I was in the middle, with Charles, now feeling pretty well, perched on my left. Talkative and energetic, he kept me thoroughly distracted by his conversation and general fidgetiness, a blessing as it turned out.

At last our extraordinary caravan was ready, and in the developing heat of midmorning we rolled out of town. At first it was so exciting to have begun, after all the preparations, waiting and ambivalence, finally to throw ourselves into it utterly, that the wretched travelling conditions did not bother us. In fact, we laughed and chattered delightedly as we drove along the reasonably adequate, if bumpy and dusty, road linking the villages spotted along the river.

After about three hours we stopped in such a village, poured out of the jeeps and had a picnic in a pasture. Here we began to realize what cramps and bruises had developed thus far, what stiffened knees and sunburned faces and arms. But lunch was good, cheese and peanuts and crackers. Villagers came to peer at us, and one of our Pakistani leaders ordered tea for us. In time it came, in little glasses on a huge tray, milky and apparently sugared, judging from all the flies. Squeamish about our health, we buzzed together about whether or not it was safe. Jock and Ray were drinking it, and said they had no trouble with tea when they travelled here, so some of us went ahead, too. I found it comforting in its warm sweetness, and closed my eyes to the flies trying to share it with me.

A couple of other villagers brought us apples, a gift, judging

22

from their friendly smiles. Again mindful of the rule about peeling any fruit, we carefully peeled these and ate them with relish.

Finally we had to go on, and groaning and complaining,rearranged ourselves on the jeeps. It was very hot now, the sun fierce through the high altitude air. Even Charles beside me was somewhat subdued, though still full of stories about school, family, adventures he had had. At one point a child stood at the side of the road with a plate loaded with grapes. Our driver, a resident of the area, knew the child, stopped the jeep, and paid a few coins for the grapes. Leaning around he gave the grapes to Charles. Sticky and coated with dust, they were not too appetizing, but we did not want to hurt the driver's feelings. We pretended to put them in our mouths, then, letting our hands trail backward, managed to drop them onto the road. It took a while but we did eventually dispose of them all.

The drive went on and on, hotter and hotter, dusty and extremely uncomfortable. The terrain was changing. The valley was narrowing, and so was the road. Now we began to negotiate cliffs, as we had on the trip up the valley from Gilgit. The river was grey with glacier water and running fast because of the rains. The cliffs dropped abruptly down to the water, and the road traversed their faces. The grafting technique of road building was prevalent here. Actually, short of carving a shelf into rock faces, there was no alternative engineering possible. Given that the road building was done with bare hands and rudimentary tools, these cliff roads were a marvel. But for those who sat on the outer sides of the jeeps, looking vertically down hundreds of feet to the river below was frightening. The rest of us were so busy flattening ourselves out so as not to be smashed in the head by the low boulders overhanging the road, that we forgot to be afraid of the road itself. Yet it was terribly tiring, dealing with these conditions, and we were relieved when, in midafternoon, the lead jeep suddenly turned off the road to cross the river for our next respite. We were not pleased with the bridge we crossed on. It was hanging on great ropes and sank under the jeep's weight, swinging majestically to and fro as we crossed. Fatigue has its advantages, however; we were too tired to panic.

Across the river was the compound and surrounding village of

23

the local Raj. It was considered a special privilege to be invited to visit him, and we had been told in advance how to behave in his presence.

We pulled into his courtyard, driving through the inevitable polo field adjacent to the compound wall. He came out to greet us, an imposing presence, a figure of the past. In his sixties, flanked by servants and children, he looked so proud and regal, that we were touched by him. Silently we filed into his reception room lined with couches, rug-covered and pillowed. Numerous photographs on the wall were of the Raj together with an assortment of visitors: military men, diplomats, world travellers. The photos dated back over the decades. Studying the memorabilia of pictures, hunting trophies, skins, vases, knickknacks, all deep in dust, I felt the awe of an ancient way, the ruthless aura of "the ruler," such an anachronism now, in this God-forsaken place.

Again tea came, again some of us accepted it gratefully, some refrained. One or two of our braver members spoke with the Raj, asking him polite questions that he answered in his modest English.

Within an hour we were loaded into the jeeps again in our tortured positions, appalled to learn that we were only halfway to our destination. There was little talk now and less joking. Now we were enduring, each of us using whatever systems we could to sustain ourselves. Mine was mainly a matter of disengaging my mind, unfortunately only partially successful since my fear of the road was so great it kept jolting me back to the immediate moment. Finally I began to think about surviving each cliff-face section and tried to determine by looking ahead how long it would be before the next one.

Sunset came, followed almost immediately by darkness. At seven o'clock we were driving by the light of the headlamps alone, and the danger of the road increased. The drivers, however, did not seem aware of this, and maintained their speed. After awhile I was simply too exhausted to be afraid. Anyway, there was something else now. What had been a relief from heat at sunset now became increasingly cold, so I could concentrate on a new misery and let the darkness blot out the horrors of the road.

24

Trekking the Hindu Kush

Late, late that evening we arrived. A walled compound appeared in front of us. This was the Rest House of Yasin, a wooden shelter composed of a large sleeping room and two bathrooms again, incredibly, with flush toilets. The shelter was being used by some Japanese mountain climbers who had been denied entrance to the back mountains and were going to have to return to Gilgit. The sinks in the bathrooms had running water, and by flashlight I washed my face, forestalling my impulse to brush my teeth with the faucet water. We were strictly on iodized water now, each of us carrying two quart-bottles which we filled at any river or irrigation ditch we could find. We had stopped a couple of times during the day at clear running rivers to fill and treat our bottles, but the clarity of the water was deceptive. We were told that the waters of the Himalayas were the most polluted in the world, since humans and animals lived their lives around the water sources. All other terrain was lifeless and savage and travelled only when in transit to another water source.

While we were cleaning up, the cooks were setting up the kitchen, and then I was introduced to the diet of the expedition. Freeze-dried something; in the darkness I could not see the label of the container it came from. Tea with milk and sugar already in it. "chappattis," a tortilla-like bread made from "atta," spread with so much grease I nearly dropped it. Well, it was dark, and I figured it must be hard to cook by the feeble kerosene lamps set up near the kitchen area. Anyway I was too tired to bother much with eating. I wiped my plate, fork and cup with a piece of the toilet paper we had brought, knowing it was pointless, but driven by habit to make order.

We then sorted ourselves out in sleeping areas outside the Rest House, stepping gingerly among the overripe apricots everywhere underfoot. Apparently apricot trees were considered good for shade, but no one had worried about the mess that the ripened, falling fruit would create. There was a lot of giggling about the squishiness, but I was somewhat concerned about the effect on our sleeping bags of being laid down on a carpet of the soft fruit.

At last the camp settled down, and we slept.

Yasin citizens supervising our activities

VI

In the morning I found out how it was that we had flush toilets.

It had been a difficult night. There was indeed great relief in stretching out in our sleeping bags, after sitting jackknifed on unyielding baggage, jolted and terrified, all day. But after the first few hours of exhausted sleep, we began to turn and shift and come awake. Though the compound seemed flat, it became clear that we were deceived in the darkness of our arrival and in fact had arranged our sleeping bags on sloping ground. Also debris of some sort on the ground became increasingly uncomfortable to lie on as we thrashed about. This, our first night in sleeping bags in a totally alien world, nine thousand feet above sea level, was difficult indeed.

After dressing awkwardly and slowly inside our bags, as one does among strangers, and going through an unfamiliar routine of washing and brushing in strange circumstances, I felt as though I had already done a morning's work, and my breath was a bit short. Also my temper.

Then I saw how the toilets worked.

Here came, across the compound, a tiny, wrinkled man. He scurried with quick steps, carrying a large pail of sloshing water. Judging from the sideways tilt of his body, the water pail was very heavy. A ladder leaned against the side of the building that housed the toilets and sinks "with running water." I realized now what the tanks on the roof were for. Sure enough, the little old man staggered painfully to the foot of the ladder, grasped it with one hand and dragged himself up its rungs, holding the bucket in his other hand. Appalled, I watched him make two more trips, then had to turn away. By now I knew how far away the nearest irrigation ditch was, and that was bad enough. But somehow the worst part was this valiant little man hauling the water up the ladder to put it in tanks, that we, spoiled Westerners, should have flush toilets.

Our first expedition breakfast was an education for what was to come. Cooks had materialized the night before from the village to make our dinner. Here they were again this morning, only now, unfortunately, one could see what they were doing. I regretted this fact at once.

Even the simplest methods of hygiene and care in food handling were ignored. Fingers, dust, bugs, grimy utensils, all went into the cooking pots. The primus stoves were set on the ground and the cooks crouched over them.

The menu itself was a challenge. A cereal with the consistency of soup, chappattis soaked in grease, "omelettes" out of powdered eggs. The omelettes were folded inside the chappattis and as you held them up to your mouth (my own hands were not wonderfully clean) the grease ran out the other end. My stomach protested, but I got it down somehow, still operating on the basis that I needed to eat for strength.

As this day proceeded some of my city attitudes began to weaken.

Yasin was the point of no return. From here we would proceed on foot north along the floor of the valley to another that intersected off to the west, toward the Hindu Raj range of the Himalayas. We were to climb a narrow, trailless canyon of rock right up to the Hindu Raj. Then we were to cross a glacier, climb over the Thui An Pass, and go down the steep descent on the other side. From there we were to cross another glacier and drop down to the head of the Yarkhun Valley. Then we were to climb another pass into the Hindu Kush range (even Jock had not scouted this route) and down the next valley to the town of Chitral at the Afghanistan border. Chitral, Gilgit, and Skardoo had the only airstrips in the western Himalayas.

There were no maps of the area from here on. No towns, only the most marginal groups of huts huddled together. Some of these had place names, but Jock cautioned us to expect nothing but curi-

28

osity from the villagers. The part of the proposed expedition that he had scouted sounded desolate as far as human comforts were concerned, and there would be an utterly unknown section beyond that.

In all, the march would be about two hundred miles, covering about ten miles every day under stiff conditions of blazing sun and 100° heat, bitter wind and cold at night, trackless moraines and cliff faces, possible floods and uncrossable rivers, and heavy storms. All of this at altitudes between nine and seventeen thousand feet.

An immediate problem was at hand, however. It had to do with our young group member Karen and her worsened physical condition. She had suffered severely the trip of the day before. This morning she was retching every ten or fifteen minutes, had a fever of several degrees, and could not hold down water. Her diarrhea continued, too, and dehydration was becoming worrisome.

After considerable discussion it was decided we would stay over an extra day. There was plenty of work to do in negotiating with local people to determine a fair price to hire their donkeys and their own services as porters. During this time it was hoped that Karen's health would improve. Since we had no medical doctor in the group, it would be very dangerous for someone in precarious health to attempt the trip. What we would do if any of us became seriously sick later, was a question no one asked.

Karen's mother, the only other woman my age, was totally preoccupied in caring for her daughter, and we all realized it was best for us to get on with our own business. So there was a general fanning out from the compound to explore.

The layout of Yasin was typical. A great river ran along the floor of the wide valley, and another came down from a narrow canyon to meet it. Our compound was near this second, smaller river. The most extraordinary feature of Himalayan villages is their irrigation system and here we had a chance fully to appreciate this construction. High up the valleys and canyons, the people would begin to dig ditches, starting at the water's edge and extending away with just enough slope to keep water flowing. They would lead these ditches down to the various fields and huts all along the valley floors. These aqueducts were perfectly maintained and were visible at great distances because poplars were often planted along them. If not poplars, grass grew alongside them, and the effect would be of long, green stripes parallel to each other and all at different altitudes. The mountains, ridges, cliff faces being traversed by the ditches were so stark and grey, so rocky and forbidding, that the green was a shock.

We sat for a long time beside the river, enjoying the warm sun, strange scenery, and multi-colored stones in the water. Villagers would come by on their way to somewhere, or just to gawk at us, and we would exchange grins and head noddings.

"Salaam," they would say, softly.

"Salaam!" we replied.

The women peered from behind their veils, the men stared openly, children gathered in groups for safety. Different age children would collect until there were six or eight of them, then they would stand or squat and watch us. After awhile we would realize that they were moving as a group nearer and nearer. It became tiring, always under surveillance like that, and either we would move away or indicate that they should. But soon they would be inching nearer again; there really was no escape from them.

Late that afternoon, by arrangement with the village leaders, a group of men came to dance for us. There was music, too, with several flutelike instruments and drums, played with great energy and enthusiasm. The dances were mainly in the precise placement of feet and graceful hand gestures. No random movements at all. The men were deliberate and constrained, yet with no sense of inhibition. Each dancer had his own steps, though there was some similarity among them all. At one point, a very small boy came out and danced with a man, perhaps his father. The boy, too, danced gravely, with a deliberate series of steps repeated over and over.

Finally, a tall old man came leaping out and put on a wild show of whirls and jumps, laughing and improvising. Perhaps with age comes freedom of expression in this so demanding country.

By the next day Karen was still sick, with no signs of recovery. Her parents were frightened now, and it was painfully decided that Karen and her mother would take the awful jeep ride back to Gilgit. There they would wait for a flight into Rawalpindi and eventually a

30

flight back to the United States, if Karen's condition permitted it. At least in Rawalpindi there was a hospital and doctors, if necessary.

The parting of mother and daughter from the rest of the family (father, brothers and their two young friends) was quiet but tear-marked. All of us were affected by their situation, and the realization that it would be weeks before either group would know of the safety of the other.

Jock and Saïd, his Pakistani assistant, Karen and her mother, the driver, luggage and food for a day, all were fitted somehow into the one jeep that had stayed with us in the event that Karen's condition deteriorated. Ray was left in charge of our group and the arrangements with cooks and porters to load and begin our march the next morning. Ray had never been here before, nor had Jahangir, the army liaison officer with us. The porters were informed that we wanted to go to Harph, the place name of a tiny village up in the canyon that intersected the valley some miles north of Yasin. Jahangir spoke Urdu, and so did the porters, though their own language was something quite different. Presumably, with these factors in our favor, we would make this next connection even without Jock or maps.

Again that night we dined on dehydrated something, drank milky tea, and went to our apricot-decorated, uncomfortable sleeping bags. The curious villagers abandoned their posts at the compound wall, where for the whole day they had stood, most of the time on tiptoe, to peer over its top and observe us at our activities.

This night was tolerable however, even with its increasingly familiar pattern of sleep for three hours then lie awake and be restless, since it looked as though, incredibly, we would actually begin to walk tomorrow.

31

A local citizen stops at sight of our group
starting out on our first day's march out of Yasin.

VII

It felt so good to be on our way, on foot, at last! At seven in the morning the air was chilly and I was glad for my parka. The sun had not yet climbed over the eastern wall of the valley. Rising another four or five thousand feet up from the river, this great ridge running north and south would block the sun for another couple of hours.

The thrill of getting started had shaken us all out of our frustrations, discomforts, and worry over Karen. Up at four-thirty, bumping around in the dark, we were hilarious and disorganized. Donkeys braying, porters shouting, Ray weighing out loads, the rest of us getting our gear packed, breakfast eaten, water bottles filled and iodized. The Japanese group came out and gazed at our preparations. They were so quiet and retiring that we hardly had known they were there, huddled most of the time inside the one building of the compound. We had no language in common, so we just grinned and nodded at each other.

As I pulled the straps of my pack over my shoulders, I had a momentary qualm. It felt heavy, though I knew it weighed scarcely ten pounds. Watching the porters struggling into their forty-pound rigs, I felt chagrined at my reaction to my own pack. Yet, I was worried. If it felt heavy now, what would it be like later? There was nothing surplus in it: the two quart bottles of water accounting for about half the weight, a tiny movie camera, lunch, a roll of toilet paper, protective face cream, and an umbrella. The umbrella had been recommended equally for rain and sun, as a supplement to a hat. Most members of the group carried an ice axe also, an item I had abandoned in Rawalpindi. Even after dragging it fifteen thousand

33

miles around the world from California, I had an intuition that I could live without it, whereas I had no such notion about the umbrella. Furthermore, the umbrella weighed perhaps one pound to the axe's three pounds, and it was clear by now that every pound was a concern.

We trooped happily out of the compound, crossed the first treacherous footbridge over the small river, and began our march. The track here was a continuation of the jeep road, though now there were only people and donkeys on it. We soon were strung out in pairs and threes along this road, chattering and cheerful. After weeks of lying around or moving in vehicles, we were finally on our way.

The other members of the group, now down to fourteen people, plus Ray and Jahangir, ranged out ahead of and behind Klaus and me, and we went along briskly like that for a couple of hours. Then the sun rose over the mountainous ridge on our right, as we proceeded north up the big valley. I opened up my umbrella and noticed that its purple silk was at striking variance with the grey surroundings. The dust on the road puffed around our feet as we walked, and the floor of the valley extended rockily away to our left, to the upward slope of the western ridge. All was grey except for the narrow green strip of vegetation on our right edging the river. My umbrella was light to handle, almost floating in the slight breeze, and I felt pleased that I had pulled it out of the back of the closet for this trip. I had had it for years, but never used it. One has little need for a purple parasol in San Francisco.

The fact was, however, that even with a hat and an umbrella, I was beginning to feel the sun. I had my small circle of shade, but all around us the air began to warm up. So did the bare ground we were walking on, and the great slopes of rock extending upward to our left. We fell silent, and concentrated on walking.

The people behind us began to catch up and pass, and we realized we were slowing down a bit. Still we were going along reasonably well, so we just grinned at the others as they went by. At the end of the third hour of steady walking, we saw a canyon coming down from the left, a narrow path angling down it to meet our road. A small river rolled down, too, crossed by a bridge at the mouth of the canyon. The road we had been walking on continued over this bridge and on up the main valley. Ray was sitting on a big rock at the intersection of path and road, swinging his legs cheerfully. He waved us toward the narrow canyon, and we were delighted to be free of the dull dusty road.

We had nearly finished our water, and we filled our bottles again in the river. We were quite pleased with ourselves for having drunk so much water—two quarts each in three hours—since Jock had made a big point about dehydration. It was surprisingly easy to drink so much water; our thirst was imperative. But at least, we felt sure, we were well ahead of any dehydration problem.

At first the walk up the path was such a pleasant change, the sun behind us now, that we speeded up. We were struck by the change in scenery. Along the walls of this narrow canyon, we were encountering many of the green stripes that denoted irrigation aqueducts. They broke up the austerity of the great ridges over our heads and offered the eye soothing attractions of grass and even occasional flowers.

Now and then, a man on a horse would come down the trail. We flattened ourselves against the cliff, worrying that the horse might shy away from such unfamiliar figures as we must have been in our Western clothes and bright colors. The path was by now high enough up the cliff face, and narrow enough that there would be little room for a horse to shy safely.

One man came along on a black horse. Again, we flattened ourselves and I closed my umbrella. The man and horse went by without change of expression, except widened eyes on both. The horse was small, elegantly proportioned, with very slim legs and a lovely head. I realized that here was a prototype of the Arabian horse so admired in the West. He carried himself lightly, head high, yet controlled. His rider, dressed in the usual cotton shirt and matching baggy pants, was as contained in his manner. Just the briefest nod, "salaam," and the widened eyes acknowledged us.

There were donkeys with their drivers on the track, too; sometimes one or two, sometimes a string of them. This was a more relaxed project, the donkeys taking any opportunity to stop and drop their heads to sniff the ground. They would look at us calmly, cranking their long fuzzy ears forward to point at us. They were endearing little beasts, unflappable and strong, usually carrying monster loads and tripping along easily on their tiny hooves.

After two or three hours of the path, we began to slacken our pace. We were simply getting tired. Neither of us had marched for five or six hours in a sustained fashion in a long time, and we were beginning to flag. We stopped to eat our lunch: pemmican, peanuts and crackers, which aggravated our thirst, so we drank up our water. Getting more was a problem. The river was a couple of hundred feet below and it did not look as though our path would cross it. Shallow irrigation ditches ran periodically alongside our path, but we were concerned about the safety of the water, given the donkey and horse droppings everywhere. Also the water seemed rather murky, and it carried along in its slow flow an alarming assortment of animate and inanimate objects.

Over the next hour or so, we tried to guess which village ahead would be Harph, our destination for the day. Villages, conglomerations of huts and cornfields, were at every bend in the river. Surely that one, or that one, would be Harph. And each time it was not.

Now the donkeys and porters for our expedition began passing us. Shouting, and swatting the donkeys with sticks, the porters went by. They gave us big grins, flashing their teeth or gums, and we became increasingly concerned.

At last Ray caught up to us, carrying what seemed to be an enormous back pack. Sweating and red in the face, he stopped for a moment.

"How much more?" we asked.

"Oh, should be just around a couple more bends," he said. "Never been here before, myself, so I don't know exactly."

We smiled at him as he went on, refraining from commenting on our failing spirits. By now, the sun was moving in front of us, early afternoon. It was becoming torturous to keep moving, with that hot sun unmediated by atmosphere flailing us. Also our feet protested their boots and our legs were trembling with fatigue. The path had begun a series of climbs and descents, so moving forward required a great deal of going up and down. The "ups" were sometimes a scramble, requiring use of hands, too, and the descents were steep enough to take the starch out of our knees. And we had run out of water.

Our stops became more frequent, and our despair mounted. Then, around a bend, we came to another irrigation ditch, with a little grass growing beside it and a string of sparse apricot trees casting a thin shade. Sitting there with his eyes popping out of a scarlet face was our group member Bob. He was a banker, and like us, led a sedentary existence. He had confided to us at Gilgit that he, too, had not prepared himself properly for this trip. He had, however, had experience in Nepal, North Africa, and other trips with this mountain agency and he hoped he would have resources to fall back on. But here he was, looking quite dreadful. He said he had just filled his bottles out of the irrigation ditch, but he felt he had better give the iodine twenty minutes or so to disinfect it properly. He did not dare to continue walking until he had some more water.

We looked at the ditch water, then at each other, then we filled our bottles, too. We waited with Bob for the iodization to take effect, glad for the excuse to sit down. I took off my boots and put my wretched feet into the ditch water. And took them out again at once. The water was icy.

"Glacier water," said Bob, watching me.

Gradually I eased my feet in, and some of the swelling did reduce.

When it came time to move on again, it required an extraordinary effort. Yet we got up, loaded on our packs and trudged onward. But we had to stop every few minutes. Not only were we exhausted, but Bob was sick. He vomited repeatedly, and looked awful. My own situation was pretty bad; my face was very hot and completely dry, even though I was drinking water constantly.

At last Bob couldn't get to his feet any more. We were frightened now. One of us would have to stay with him while the other struggled on to find the camp and assistance. I was only too glad to stop there, and Bob and I settled to wait. Actually, after a while, he and I did manage to proceed for a little distance, stop again, proceed. But it was at a snail's pace, and the sun was merciless.

At last we heard familiar voices, and four of the younger people appeared. They simply infused us with energy and renewed hope, and half supporting, half dragging, nagged us on to the campground.

It was about three-thirty when we arrived. The relatively cool campground was actually an orchard of the inevitable apricot trees. It was out of the sun, down near the river, and best of all, we could stop walking.

We shrugged slightly as we unrolled our sleeping bags on another carpet of fallen, squashy fruit. We were beginning to be less fussy.

VIII

Bob was very sick all evening. Lying on his side, curled up into himself, he retreated. He could keep nothing down, vomiting up even the tea that was brought to him. Finally we left him alone.

The rest of us lounged around, in various states of fatigue. No one, except Bob, was felled by heat exhaustion, though there were a few of us who came close. My extremely dry, hot skin returned to normal as I drank the tea, iodized water, and lemonade that were constantly pressed on me.

Charles showed me the advantages offered by the adjacent cornfield. Given that we were always in a group, and always under the fascinated scrutiny of the local people, it was difficult to arrange for the more personal functions of the body. Charles, who seemed to know everything about mountaineering, went trooping off with his roll of toilet paper right into the heart of the head-high corn. All one could see was the top of his head and the movement of the stalks. Then his head disappeared, and the stalks stopped moving until a few minutes later when he reappeared.

This system worked well for me, too, and I began to feel a small confidence growing. Part of what was so fatiguing about the previous couple of weeks was the strangeness. Even the simplest routines had to be re-thought and arranged for. One realizes only then how much energy is freed by developing patterns of behavior that maintain themselves without conscious attention.

Just to see about morning ablutions involved collecting one's water bottle, properly iodized, toothbrush, paste, towel, soap, comb, and toilet paper, and finding a spot reasonably removed from the rest of the group. I was forever forgetting something, or dropping something. But mainly, it was the mental effort to organize myself anew and invent a system every time that I found wearing.

At six o'clock the next morning it was daylight. The air was sharp and cold, so we dressed in sweaters and parkas. With little atmosphere to modify the temperature, there was a startling change from hot to cold to hot. In the sun, the heat was terrible, more than the one-hundred degree temperature would justify. The immediacy of the sun made the difference. When the sun went behind the mountains at five or so in the afternoon, the air turned cold at once. One of the rude conditions of the Himalayas is the close proximity of opposites, and not only in respect to temperatures.

Pulling ourselves together, this early morning in Harph, involved much concern with feet. Mine were not bad since my boots fit well, but I did have extensive light blisters all over the soles of my feet from sheer mileage. Beth, young and sympathetic, had had much mountain experience, and she insisted I apply "moleskin," a thin sponge, adhesive on one side, to the bottoms of my feet.

"Just leave it on until it falls off by itself," she said briskly.

Klaus's feet were bad. They were raw in many places, even bloody, and severe blisters were on his toes and heels. But it was Tom, in his borrowed boots, who was in the worst trouble. Huge blood blisters and raw flesh were everywhere on his feet. He and Klaus decided to forego boots and wear low shoes. The only such shoes Klaus had were loafers; Tom borrowed a pair of tennis shoes. He had to cut out the toes of the shoes so that the blood blisters could stick out. He still had to hobble.

We ate breakfast. Hunger was beginning to overrule the palate. I began to develop a taste for the runny cereal and the sweet tea, though the chappattis and omelettes still made me too queasy to eat.

What with the foot problems and the general inefficiency of a new group, we did not begin our day's march until about eight o'clock. The sun was beginning to rise over the mountainous ridges behind us as we headed on up the narrow valley. Actually, to my

40

great surprise, I felt pretty good again. Restless or not, I had been refreshed by the night. Now I could look about me and take an interest in my strange circumstances.

The path, somewhat rockier today than yesterday, ran along the river, up on the steep slope about one or two hundred feet. As it had done in the lower part of the canyon yesterday, it proceeded in sharp ascents and descents, though overall it was climbing steadily. The vegetation and plantings along the river became discontinuous. More and more the rocky fall of the ridge would extend right down to the river. Frequent clusters of apricot trees along the path, however, provided some shade. After hesitating initially over the "safety" issue, we finally began simply to help ourselves freely to the overhanging fruit. It was only partly ripe, having something of the taste and consistency of apples, but juicy and refreshing, nonetheless.

On great boulders above and below the path apricots were spread out to dry in the sun, hot orange colored, and thoroughly speckled with dirt and flies. These we left alone.

After a couple of hours, I was no longer so fresh. The path became increasingly exposed to the sun, as we left behind villages and crops. The two in city shoes began to struggle with the rocks on the path, and the path itself began to narrow as we got higher.

Finally, below us, far down the slope, we saw a footbridge crossing the river. On the other side, in the shade of an overhanging cliff, sat three or four advance members of our group. Obviously, we were to leave the main path here and cross to the other side. Which we did, moving fast across the rickety bridge so as not to let fear take over. It was quite high in the air over a rough river in a boulder-choked bed. Resting for a bit with the others, we checked our condition. Some pain for a few, especially those with hurt feet, and some anxiety about a recurrence of heat exhaustion for Bob, but all in all, things were going quite well.

Jahangir, one of those resting, said, "Well, today is a short day; we should get to Muishk in a few hours."

I was glad to know our next camp and place name, figuring that meant conditions would be comparable to last night's, i.e., tolerable. But in the direction we were to proceed, all looked pretty forbidding. Irrigation ditches still traced their green way across the barren ridges before us, but there seemed to be little else growing.

"How high do you think we are?" I asked Jahangir.

"I don't know," he said in his hard to understand accent. "Perhaps ten thousand feet. It's maybe another thousand feet up in Muishk."

We had gotten this far before noon, about halfway apparently. So I felt quite brave and competent as we started off again. By the time we had marched another three hours, I was on the ropes and there was no sign of Muishk. The terrain had opened out onto a plain, moonlike with dust and scattered rocks in all directions, scorching in the sun. There was not much opportunity to look around, however, because the path kept disappearing.

"Here's a boot print," one of us would say.

Only three or four of us were together during this part, most of the others having gone ahead out of view. The experience of the day before began again. The hopeless feeling that we would not make it at all was aggravated by the fact that we did not know how much farther we had to go. It was clear that we were to continue in this direction. Up ahead we could see that the valley narrowed again, but we had to expend precious energy picking out the path through the loose rock. We could not gear ourselves to an estimated time or distance.

Jahangir's statement about "a short day" infuriated us. Maybe for him and the experienced ones, but certainly not for those of us who were less trained. The huge sun and blazing heat was debilitating. Even if we had not ached in every muscle and joint, the frying action of the sun was overwhelming.

Perhaps we were delirious, because a bizarre incident occurred to which we could not respond as we normally would. We came to an apparently inhabited area with dense hedgerows, a few mangy poplars, and glimpses of rough huts. As we marched along one of the hedgerows, a man suddenly popped out of the bushes to stand in front of us. Gesturing widely, he nodded and grinned at us.

"You come have tea," he said in English. "You come have tea! I am PIA salesman. I have tea for you."

42

Frank, a New Zealander in our group, responded as we gawked, "Thank you, yes, yes, I'll come for tea."

Shaking our heads, in a daze, Klaus and I simply went on up the path. To our unease we saw Frank go off with the Pakistan Airlines fellow.

We were too sun-drugged and exhausted to discuss it. We just plodded on and on through the dust and rock, looking up only to make sure we were going in the right direction.

An endless interval later, Frank, in excellent condition for all his sixty years, caught up with us. He talked cheerfully of his tea visit. We did not care, did not listen, and ceased recording our experience.

A while later I came to consciousness enough to realize we were sitting on the slimy bank of an irrigation ditch with our feet in its equally slimy water.

Eventually we found the others of our group, gathered in the shade of some strange, sparse trees. This was Muishk, a flat area with a few trees and bushes, and a meandering marshy stream.

No people at all, apparently.

We fell down under a tree and lay without moving. Someone shoved water at us, so we drank it, not caring.

A long while later we began to sit up and take stock. The heat was ebbing, and there was more shade. But the condition of our feet was worrisome, and I saw to my great concern that my edema had increased. What had been a relatively minor matter of shapeless ankles and fat fingers, now was more like elephantiasis. My legs were swollen up to my knees, hot and throbbing. My wrists were fat and spongy, and I could feel that my face was affected, too. Just as well there were no mirrors around.

What would happen as we got higher? I was poorly informed on edema, knowing only that the pulmonary type could lead to quick death. Ray seemed not too concerned, but he was not making any guarantees either. The thought of trying to make my way back over the distance we had already covered left me appalled. So I soaked the scarves Beth loaned me in the cold water, tied them around my swollen legs, and tried not to think about it.

Camp was set up by late afternoon, and there was much laughing and chattering among the porters and donkey owners. Staring moodily at the scene, I could scarcely believe that these thin, small people could still have so much energy. So when they began to play polo on their donkeys, I watched wonderingly. Using long sticks cut from bushes, and some soft wadded-up material as a ball, they kicked at their donkeys and milled around. Charles climbed on a donkey and joined in, his long, skinny fifteen-year old legs hanging to the ground. The donkeys, tiny little animals, had carried their great loads all day, in awful heat, and now were called upon to play polo. If I had cared about anything at that point, I suppose I would have felt badly for them. Yet they did not seem to be suffering; with their ridiculous ears waving forward and back, tails switching energetically, they seemed to enter into the spirit of the game.

Soon my grumpiness and general sense of horror at my situation yielded a bit, and the unlikeliness of it all took over. It was a weird and funny scene, and I relaxed and enjoyed it.

44

IX

At dawn, a porter brought Jahangir his tea. As a captain in the Pakistani Army, he expected service and got it. Awakened out of my usual half-sleep by this transaction, I propped myself up on my elbows to look around. Jahangir was sitting up, sipping his tea. He smiled across at me and I grinned back. I was always glad when the night was over.

Then I saw that there were two more sleeping bag humps than last night. Jock and Saïd had caught up with us, apparently. I was thoroughly impressed as I realized what a great distance they had had to make up. Whatever I thought of Jock personally, there was no doubt about his mountaineering capacity.

I gestured toward the humps, looking at Jahangir, and he nodded.

At breakfast we learned that Jock and Saïd had gotten in about two in the morning, walking the last few hours by moonlight. They had escorted Karen and her mother to Gilgit and onto the plane for Rawalpindi the next morning. Karen had begun to feel better by then, and it seemed likely that the two women would fly back to California within a day or two.

Jock and Saïd had been driven by jeep straight through from Gilgit, past Yasin, to the intersection of the northern valley road and the canyon where we had all turned west two days ago. They had proceeded up the path we had climbed to where we were now, with only the briefest of stops to sleep and eat. And here they were this morning looking fit and rested. The contrast between them and the two of us was wide.

We two and Tom had decided the night before that we would try for a very early start this morning. The track ran north and south for the next few miles and if we began early we would have several hours before the sun climbed over the east wall of the narrow valley. The valley walls were still in the form of razor-topped ridges, about fifteen thousand feet high, and lying in this direction, cast a morning shade.

We settled for tea for breakfast, not wanting to wait for the cereal to be cooked, collected bags of peanuts and pemmican for lunch, and took off. Behind us, the energetic voices of porters circled around Jahangir. Complicated negotiations were going on for the next stage of the march. Since the donkeys could go no farther—the terrain and the altitude would be too much for them—the equipment and baggage would all have to be carried from here by porters. This would mean increasing the number of carriers to manage the gear carried by the fifteen or so donkeys we had been using.

In this part of the Himalayas there were no professional porters, as contrasted with Nepal, for instance. These men were local villagers, and they would not march more than a day or two away from their homes. As a result, Jahangir had frequently to negotiate for new porters. The advantage to this system was that all porters were used to the thin air of their own areas and could carry maximum loads, as much as two-thirds of their own weight.

Tom's feet in their tennis shoes, and Klaus's in their loafers, were barely making it. Their blisters had broken by now, and they were making extensive use of bandages and moleskin. Yet, in the cold morning air, they seemed optimistic enough.

We headed up the faint trail and soon found ourselves climbing up a great rockfall. It was a bit tricky because the rocks were unstable and it would be easy to break an ankle or leg if a rock turned underfoot. We were fresh, though, and the two men carried their ice axes while I carried my umbrella for balance.

After an hour of climbing we stopped to look back, and our hearts sank. There, strung out in single file, were the miniature figures of our group, skirting around the base of our rockfall. In our ignorance we had missed the lower trail and followed an upper one unnecessarily. Cursing the waste of precious shade time and energy, we picked our way back down the fall. By angling down and across we retained some forward progress, but it was discouraging nonetheless to find ourselves in the middle of the group once again.

Still, the air was cool and the path ascended relatively little, so we could make good time. We were crossing a plateau above the river and the path was clear and rock-free. I began to find a walking rhythm, something like an overdrive gear in a car.

After a while we three were alone. Those ahead of us had disappeared around a long curve of the valley, and the slower people were falling ever farther behind. Greenhorns or not, city shoes or not, we began to feel some satisfaction in our capacity.

By ten o'clock the sun was clear of the ridge and coming down on us hard. As we approached the end of the north-south track, we were presented with a harsh, albeit impressive scene. A great ridge wall wedged down into the valley, splitting it into two forks, east and west, each with its glacier river. The area of the intersection was wide open, a huge flat terrain of rocks extending out all around us, glaring at us in the hot sun. A hostile sight.

We knew we were to take the east fork, crossing the river by means of a skimpy bridge. Like all the other bridges we had seen until now, this one was made first of a row of thin tree trunks laid across the river, propped up at either end on piles of rock. Even thinner branches were laid crosswise over them, with twigs and big rocks added to fill the gaps, and more rocks laid on top to step on while crossing. The bridge was scarcely wider than the narrow stepping strip and without railings. It was necessary to begin the crossing with one's whole attention focussed on the other side. If you concentrated on each step you were lost, and the fall some twenty feet down to the fast river below with its rough boulders would have caused much breakage. You looked at your feet just enough to see that they were placed properly, but your energy was devoted always to the next step ahead, never the present one.

We found a note sticking out from under a rock on the other side saying to proceed up this fork of the river, and giving the hour and names of the others of our group who had passed by earlier. We stood here, feeling the terrible sun not only above, but glaring up at us from the rocks we stood on. The east fork extended narrowly ahead of us. There was no track across the rocks; we would have to pick our way over them.

Suddenly we heard a shout from the left. A character looking like a refugee from the Old Testament came over a slight rise of rocks.

"Chai! Chai!" he shouted. Far behind him we could see a flat roofed hut, slate colored, and set low into the rocks. In our fatigue and heat bewilderment, we stared at each other and at the apparition in flapping garments waving wildly at us. We wanted no part of it. All that mattered now was to get to the next camp and away somehow from the sun.

"No, no, thank you! No tea, my wife is sick! We have to go on!" Klaus shouted back, not knowing if the words would be understood in this extraordinary part of the world. Our fear and distress was so great that we included this man in it, figuring he meant to capture us or poison us.

Leaving the man calling and waving, feeling guilty and anxious, we began to trudge across the rocks to the beginning of the fork. It was exhausting to find our footing, every step had to be determined carefully since the rocks were loose and rolled when our weight came down on them, and we had to invent our own way over them. When we got into the fork, we found ourselves following a river bed, mercifully dry except for a small river on one side. Thus we could ascend gradually. But the heat and fatigue were just too much for me, and I sat down and cried. Worried, Klaus sat down, too, gave me some of his water and sympathized. But there was nothing to do but go on. Which, after a while, we did.

Around a bend in the river bed we saw that the canyon was narrowing now so much that the river filled the bottom of it, and we would have to climb up its side. There was, as usual, a rock slope up from the river to the ridge above. All was, also as usual, unstable and ready to roll. We realized that these slopes had no dirt to hold the rocks, and that very little would be needed to dislodge their perilous arrangement. We climbed gingerly up this rock slide and found a suggestion of a track, perhaps made by goats. Not a path, but periodic droppings. We began to look for these droppings, and found that it was easier to pick our way over the rock when we did. Perhaps use by the goats had settled the rocks a bit. It was hard to keep to the goat track, however. Whenever there was too much distance between droppings, we would wander off the track, such as it was, and it would take searching to find it again.

All this was very hard on the feet, and Tom began to fall farther and farther behind. In order to be able to go at all, I had to go at my natural speed, so Klaus and I kept going ahead until we were finally quite alone. In the heavy heat and unrelieved rock of this narrow canyon, we had the eerie sense of being lost. Except for each other, everything was strange and rejecting. This place did not want us, and we did not want it. It was a complete estrangement from everything. Looking at Klaus's face, I could see my dismay mirrored there.

Then we came upon an astonishing scene. On the other side of the canyon, a glacier hung low, with a great tube of water falling from underneath it. We realized then that we had been hearing the thunder sound of the water for some while, but had not noted it. We stared up at the glacier, following its bulk to the top of the ridge. There was snow up there, and we realized that at last we were in the Himalayas. Ahead of us ranged snow peak after snow peak, massive couloirs, frozen white and pure, tilted steeply down toward us. This was the Hindu Raj range; we were stunned by its awesome presence.

After a while we continued and in time came to a huge overhanging boulder which offered some shade. We crawled under it to rest and drink water. From here we could watch the glacier with its waterfall, and know at last why we had come on this terrible trip.

At last, we were venturing into the vast corridors and towers of these mystical mountains. It was to explore for ourselves this magic realm that we had pushed ourselves past our usual physical limits. At our ages, it was now or never. We had little to say, or think; we were just there, immersed in heat and the sound of thunder.

A rock tumbled nearby, and I looked that way, startled. A

goat's head appeared, with its beard projecting briskly forward from its chin. Horns and yellow eyes, all very near. He looked at me, fierce and proud, and came the rest of the way into view. Soon there were dozens of goats, swarming past us on all sides, their sharp little hooves, cloven, gripping the rocks.

We heard a shout, and again an apparition appeared from the Bible. Wrapped in skins from head to foot, came a wild man, shouting and throwing rocks at his herd. We watched, fascinated, as they passed. The man looked right at us, with no indication that he saw us, yet I know he did. Perhaps we were as impossible for him as he was for us.

Some while later we pulled ourselves together and, without talking, proceeded on our way, stepping and struggling through the heat and brilliance of the day. An endless time after that we arrived at the next camp. We were told that it, too, had a place name, Shotaling, but we saw only a flat rocky space beside the river, surrounded on three sides by frightening snow peaks.

X

Shotaling is like the bottom of a bucket placed up on a high shelf, a bucket partly filled with rough rocks averaging the size of grapefruit.

We climbed up the steep, stony cliffs to a breach in the side of the bucket and collapsed like corpses on the slightly tilted circle that was its bottom. Lying on our backs any which way, we saw nothing at first. I heard, dispassionately, my own gasping and sighing. I was beyond caring about my image and was glad to accept water from someone of the little group of people who had arrived there before us. I still had a little water of my own, but the effort to fish it out of my pack was not possible.

I hurt everywhere, but the worst was the feeling of having used my last reserves of energy. How would I ever muster enough to go again the next day? Fear was with me all the time. What if I couldn't make it? If I could no longer put one foot in front of the other? I could no longer go back, but what was ahead? The edema was getting very severe. It was all through my system, and I worried that damage would be done if I kept pushing on. Yet what option was there?

Finally I felt enough strength return to sit up and pull off my boots. And to look where I was.

It was indeed like being at the bottom of a bucket. Except for the narrow breach through which we had approached, we were shadowed by a great circle of utterly forbidding rock slabs leaping up yet higher to great snow-plastered points and peaks. It was terrible the way the snow was glued to the jagged, toothy towers hanging over us. As if it could all come crashing down on us at any moment.

One wall was a massive glacier, pouring ice and water down into our "bucket," creating a river that smashed by us full of ice chunks. It was a totally consuming scene, and none of us could say much about it. We just sat there silently, staring, and drinking our water. This was the Hindu Raj range, and we were at its mercy.

It was midafternoon and the sun had long since been eclipsed by the great wall of mountains, so it was getting very cold. The porters had not yet arrived with our gear, so we had to make do with the light parkas we had with us. We were lucky that there was no wind to speak of.

It was a barren campsite. Not one living thing besides us, except for two or three little clumps of tiny trees shivering together. No more than ten or twelve feet high, with skimpy foliage, they were nonetheless a comfort to the eye in all the rockiness. There was no sign of animal life, not even an insect or a bird. There was not even any dirt. These mountains, rocks and rivers seem to have been thrust up from the molten center of the earth, then frozen at once like a shriek. There was something uncanny about them. We were intruders and had better watch out for our lives.

Some timeless interval later, probably only a few minutes, the porters began to straggle in. The rest of our group appeared in twos and threes, speechless and exhausted. We found our duffles and tried to make ourselves comfortable for the night. That was, of course, not possible, but we two did commandeer one of the little clumps of trees. There was even a suggestion of privacy, which we realized only then how much we had missed. Frank, the New Zealander travelling by himself, asked if he could share our clump of trees. We agreed, but were disappointed to have to relinquish the precious separation. A sensitive man, and experienced about such things, he found somewhere else to spread out his sleeping bag. We did sit together and talk for a while, and out of our appreciation of him we confided our fear of what lay ahead. He decided to scout the next day's trip and with us gawking after him, marvelling at his physical resources, he disappeared up a cliff.

Suddenly, as if hit by lightning, I experienced a hunger panic. I felt completely, inexplicably, frantic about the lack of meat or cheese

52

or other solid protein, and it hit me all at once that I must get something. Now.

Ray had appeared and was helping the porters unpack their great packs. I went to him, interrupting his work and feeling badly about doing so. Yet my panic was of such proportions that I was compelled. Taking a look at me, Ray produced a can of cheese and handed it to me without discussion.

I scuttled away with the cheese, like a starving animal, and brought it back to where we had spread out our gear. The two of us wolfed down a whole one pound can of cheese in minutes.

Or rather, I did, having far more than my share. I did calm down then, and thought wonderingly of the power of that panic. Again, I was shocked at my utter inexperience. What business did I have being locked away in this tiny round place underneath all those awful mountains?

We went to the howling river to fill our water bottles, and almost could not do it. Timorously, we crouched on a flat boulder at its edge and dipped our bottles into the water. But it was piling past us so fast and was so ice-filled that it threatened to knock our bottles out of our hands. I thought, what if I fell in? I'd be smashed on the rocks in a moment. After trying a few times, we did, however, get our bottles partly filled, and were glad to back away from the river.

We got back to our camp to find it overrun with goats. Extraordinary little beasts, they were running through everyone's belongings, pawing and nibbling at clothes, sleeping bags, toiletries. We shouted at them, threw rocks, and they just shook their bearded heads, threatened us with their horns and did as they pleased.

After a few minutes of bedlam, the goatherder appeared from nowhere and laced into his herd. Laying about him with a stick, kicking and pushing them, shouting and rock-throwing, he shoved them through our camp and on down the canyon. In a moment they were gone, and we stood around dazed. This place was crazy, and we were stunned by it.

Then Frank reappeared and described what he had seen. Above our heads was a vast snow and ice bridge across the river, leading up to the glacier that formed one side of the wall around us.

He seemed to think it would be sound enough for us to cross over it. He said the climb up to the snow bridge was perhaps one thousand feet, and beyond that he could not see. From what Jock told us, though, he assumed that we could follow the glacier up the valley to Thui An Pass, since it seemed that the glacier flowed down to Shotaling from the pass.

I groaned and worried aloud about how I was going to get up the thousand feet of cliff to the snow bridge, let alone make the march up the glacier. Frank offered cheerfully to lead me up, saying that I could follow closely behind him and that he would see that I made it. Touched, I agreed to his suggestion and felt somewhat comforted.

The evening followed its usual pattern of dinner at dusk, eating reconstituted macaroni and cheese and pudding out of a coffee cup with a spoon. Standing around the cooks, bundled and muffled against the cold, we were a strange crew, quiet and reflective. People soon disappeared to their rocky beds, and the night fell down on us.

XI

In the morning Jock told us that the cook was sick, with a fever of 103 degrees. Other people were sick, too, but it was not the same sort of worry. They did not, after all, have their hands in our food as the cooks did. The assistant cooks put on breakfast all right, but as we stood by the primus stoves eating cereal out of our cups, we were conscious of the blanketed hump that was the head cook.

Jock was upset. He had scolded the porters and cooks the night before for not having brought warm clothes. There was at least a twenty-degree greater drop in temperatures when the sun went down here at twelve thousand feet than at the eight and nine thousand foot level, where these men lived. People in this area of the Himalayas had no reason to climb up into the mountains past the last village. They were unfamiliar with the contrasts of temperature above them.

Each porter had only his thin cotton garment and a light blanket for the night, and it was not enough. Now we could see Hussein, the sick cook, as Jock went over to speak to him. The tiny dark man poked his head out of his blanket. We could see that he was wrapped in a jacket Jock had given him and had on his head the inevitable Hunza cap that all men wore in these mountains. These plus his blanket could not have kept him warm through the bitter night just past.

Jock came back to us to say that he would stay with the cook for a day, and perhaps catch up with us the next day. He considered Hussein his friend; they had made part of this same trip together last year when Jock was scouting the route. As such, he felt he should be the one to stay back. Ray would lead us through the next stage.

This was fine with us. Ray was the real leader anyway. Jock's work was scouting and photography; Ray took care of us.

We rolled up our gear, turned it over to Ray for apportionment among the porters, and left the campsite to face what was next.

The first job was to scale a nearly vertical cliff face of several hundred feet. Frank came for me as he promised and I attached myself to his heels. I put my boot on each step as he left it. The footing was adequate here; one could place one's feet safely. But the ascent was inexorable. Like climbing stairs, hundreds of them, no stopping, lift your knee, place your foot, push off with the other foot, and repeat. Over and over again.

I looked only at Frank's heels. Saw nothing else but the lifting of his heel, the step waiting for my boot, then looked to his other heel as it lifted. Perhaps it was only an hour or so. I had switched off my mind and was in psychic neutral, focussed only on my feet and legs.

At the top of the cliff Frank stopped and I almost bumped into him. He grinned at me, and we stood for a while looking down on the campsite. There were still quite a few small figures moving around preparing to leave. I did not envy them the cliff. From up here the barren space, Shotaling, was as nothing. No more than the head of a tortured, narrow slash in the mountains. A geographical point, that's all.

The power was in the massive encirclement of mountains, piled up on each other, filling the horizon all around us. Most of them were ten or twelve thousand feet above us, great shafts and cliffs of rock, ice, and snow sticking up into the clear sky. It was not just that we were at twelve or thirteen thousand feet ourselves, and that the peaks rose nearly as high again above us. It was mainly the disturbing effect of those towering shafts being fully visible, all those thousands of feet extending from where we stood straight up to their pinnacles above our heads.

Frank and I turned to cross the thick snow bridge that began here. It groaned and creaked deep inside its heart as we picked our way over it. The snow was dirty and full of rocks. A few inches down we could see the ice, also full of pebbles and rocks and dirty. It had a glassy look and developed cracks as we stepped on it. Here the rocks were a blessing, giving us good traction on a surface that would otherwise have required crampons.

I was glad to get off the bridge. In my ignorance I had no confidence in its capacity to hold our weight.

On the other side we were faced with a huge tumble of rocks and boulders, shoved in heaps by the action of the glacier above us. There was no path through this; we had to clamber over it all to get to the glacier. Again I focussed on Frank's feet as he hopped and jumped from rock to rock. It was a matter of luck to jump on a rock that stayed put. It was just as likely to roll underfoot and cause a fall.

After a while I began to notice differences between rocks that were stable and those that might roll, and my speed grew with increasing confidence. In fact I began to enjoy this hopping and jumping, reminded of my childhood years of doing this same thing for fun. For those who had never played in rocks, this section was miserable and slow. Klaus in his loafers and Tom in his tennis shoes were wretched here and fell far behind Frank and me. Survival was of the first importance, however, and I elected to stick with Frank this day. Jock had described this section of the march as tough, the first time he recognized our efforts that way. Given how tough all the days had been for me until now, I was very worried about what lay between me and the next campsite.

We came to a small slope of snow after the rockfall, and again stopped to rest and look back. Our passage was marked by those behind us, a procession of tiny, moving color-spots, snaking like a string of beads down the whole distance. They scarcely looked like people at all to me, perhaps because people were such an anomaly in this impossible scenery. I felt we should have been forbidden entrance here.

But again we pushed on. We were getting onto the glacier now, all ice with a veneer of rocks and pebbles. Like the snow bridge, it groaned and creaked, and sometimes the glassiness crazed as we stepped on it. For a time I was fascinated; I had never been on a glacier before and I found it a remarkable experience.

We came to the first crevasse, which lay across our path. I peered cautiously over the edge into its icy opening. It was a narrow slit, but the interior dropped out of sight. Frank jumped over it, then turned to offer me the handle of his ice axe. I grabbed hold and jumped. It was a distance of only a couple of feet, but there was something terrifying about it. How deep did it go?

This was just the first of dozens of crevasses to come, and I began to dread their appearance. More often than not it was necessary to go around them, or to look for a narrow point where one could jump over. Each detour delayed us and used up precious energy. Frank began to feed me hard candies and pressed milk biscuits. They were invaluable for sustaining my strength, and I tried to repay him by keeping up with him.

In fact we were doing well in relation to the whole group, and I derived energy from that knowledge. Green or not, I was well forward in the middle between the fastest and slowest people. Only the porters kept passing us. Frank commented on this and told me that many of them were in a hurry because they were going to go back for a second trip. Even with extra porters, the loss of the donkeys left us short of carriers. It was by now only about midmorning and the thought of having to repeat any of it was intolerable. I watched the wiry, small men as they passed us so easily. How could they be so strong given their impoverished diet and exhausting existence?

By now, the sun was pounding on our backs and heads. I held up my purple umbrella, but it was little protection from that hot pressure. The heat and glare was even worse than usual since it was coming up from the glacier, too. Glasses and squinting were puny gestures; there was nothing to do but keep marching.

The glacier rose ahead of us to perhaps fourteen thousand feet, a wide frozen river between two tall walls of mountain. We zigged and zagged from side to side, detouring crevasses, ascending and descending small ridges that had been thrust up by the accordion action of the glacier. We trudged ever up and up, and grew ever groggier in the thin air and punishing heat.

Water began to collect on the surface of the glacier; the sun was melting the ice. The creaking and groaning underfoot increased, and the slipperiness, too. I became more careful of my footing after I slipped and fell a couple of times. Here and there were big pools of just barely melted water, and steep icy slopes that led down to black pools with pieces of ice floating in them.

I became completely disengaged from the surroundings; nothing existed but Frank's boots ahead of me, marching, marching. I was closed into myself, without thought or feeling, a closed inner world of silence and solitude. It was as if I had become disembodied, a hollow shell being towed up the glacier by Frank's boots.

Gradually the ice lessened and the rocks increased. We were leaving the body of the glacier and beginning to traverse its moraine. Again we were confronted by heaps of loosely piled rocks, ready to roll at a touch. There was no fun this time, however, fatigue was too great, and the rocks went on forever. We could not see where they ended. They seemed to rise steadily for a long way, then fall away or level out. Our vantage point was too low to determine how much more we had to go. So often this had been the case: the lift of hope that we were almost there, only to come around a bend and see nothing but more march to endure. So it was this day. Scrambling up a long heap of rocks, only to see rank upon rank of rock ridges rise in front of us, mostly at right angles to our direction. Falling, rolling down the other side, only to have again to scramble up the next ridge. It was like being in a boat on a sea of rock-waves.

It did, of course, stop finally, this long, long section of moraine, after one last, difficult area where the rock was heaped without pattern. Our course was nearly aimless, guided only by the great walls on either side. We wandered all over that last area of moraine, lost in its ridges and valleys.

When we did finally come to the end of it, we saw that the people who had been ahead of us and out of our sight, had stopped on a side hill on a reasonably level spot. Obviously they were waiting for us there. Our hopes leaped: perhaps this was our next campsite. It was early afternoon now, and the sun was at its worst. It would be wonderful to stop.

To get where they were sitting turned out to be difficult, too. The last part of the slope against which the moraine had ground its way, was a chewed-up mass of rock that slid away from every step. It was like trying to climb a sand dune. Somehow, though, with the promise of the campsite just at hand, we were inspired to extra effort. By churning our feet as fast as we could, we inched always a little forward and up, angling our way across the scree. The expenditure of energy was devastating, and when we finally threw ourselves onto the knoll where the others were sitting, we were like fish flopping on the shore, gasping and struggling for oxygen.

After awhile, when our hearts began to beat at a more reasonable rate, and we could breathe more easily, we asked about our campsite. Oh no, we were told, this isn't it, it's quite a bit more. It would be necessary to climb over a large hill and then back down again to the river bed; Jock had described an enormous rock there that we would camp against.

Frank and I looked at each other, and I felt the anger of despair. It sounded like several more hours, and a considerable ascent as well. I could see no possibility of making it that much farther. We decided to wait for Klaus and Tom, whom we could see still struggling across the moraine in their ridiculous shoes, and then decide what to do next.

The others nodded, wished us luck, and started off again.

XII

It was painful and yet interesting to watch Klaus lead Tom through the maze of rock ridges below us. It was like being a giant experimenter watching mice try to pick their way through a labyrinth. The glacier lay in an east-west direction, and the crevasses and ridges lay across it, north-south. So the two small figures below us had to travel along the ravines that tended to go in the direction of the glacier rather than across it. From where we sat, we could see the best route for them to take, and shouted and gestured to them accordingly. But the distance was too great, and the wind carried our voices away.

They plugged along, zigging and zagging their way up the glacier. Too often they had to clamber over the rock ridges, and we winced for their poor feet. Too often one or the other would step on a loose rock and stumble forward or fall.

Then came the scree, and the dunelike slippage of climbing up the steep slope to where we were sitting. They sat down, speechless with fatigue, and emptied their shoes. For a while we just sat together quietly.

Soon, though, the forces of hunger, heat, and sun drove us to pull out our food and water and prop my purple umbrella up on an ice axe to provide a small spot of shade. We gathered around this spot and had lunch.

The realization that we still had far to go to the next camp cast a dark mood over us. From our position we could look back over the great Anghost Bar glacier we had just traversed, and the sight subdued us. We were too little. Four people alone in an enormous landscape. There was now no one in view at all, though we knew that there were still people behind us. The massive black and white glacier stretched out like a restless animal below us. The black rock spears and the thrusting fingers of snow peaks looming all around us had a ferocious quality. Again I felt we were intruding.

In the whole black and white scene, we four were the color in our bright reds and greens, shaded by my purple umbrella. We could not stand up to our surroundings as bravely as our colors did, however. As we pulled ourselves up to continue the march, we hunched together against the landscape.

Trudging up a steep switchback of a track, following the boots in front of me, I retired even more into myself. One foot, the other foot; the sun was fierce on my head, even through the umbrella shield. I became disembodied again. I felt nothing under my boots; the strain in my legs and the pain in my shoulders from the pack belonged not to me. I floated inside myself, without thought or consciousness, suspended in space. Everything went still, and I was no longer a person—just a sense of continuity, a spot flowing along.

Consciousness returned with the sudden awareness of greenery, flowers, and pale blue butterflies. We were traversing a round hill that was rilled by small streams bubbling down over rocks. It was a shock to see this color and cheerfulness, especially when a quick look around confirmed that the mountains and glacier were still there.

It was as if the Garden of Eden had been opened to us in the midst of that sun-tortured yet frozen hell. The sun seemed less vicious with the green grass and shrubs to absorb it and the clear little waterfalls to sing to it. Here, at perhaps fifteen thousand feet, after miles of terrain with no living thing in it, not a blade of grass nor insect nor bird, here was a garden with pale blue butterflies fluttering from flower to flower.

We stopped and saw each other again. Pain returned, and I knew my body once more. It hurt and was drained by fatigue. I could only know that I had arrived in Eden; I could not make further use of the scene. Still, the sharp contrast between this colorful sight and the aggression of all the rest of the terrain had done its job of initiating consciousness, and I remained embodied.

Finally the path began to descend briskly and we left the green hill to return to rocks again, this time laid out in the form of a partly dry river bed. Again, no dirt, no sand, no living thing. All there was, down in the bend of the river at the foot of the hill, was a great block of stone the size of a large house standing alone on the dry bed, casting a bit of shade on one side. Clustered around in this shade were the figures of those who had gone ahead. Many porters had already unloaded and the cooks had their pots set up. Sleeping bags were laid out over the rocks, and people were going back and forth between the camp and the river, where it flowed some distance away on the outer rim of the bend. On the far side of the great rock, rising straight up like an amphitheater was the rockfall that constituted Thui An Pass. We would have to climb this great mass in order to cross from the Hindu Raj range over to the Hindu Kush.

As we made our way down to the river and our next camp, we resented the loss of precious altitude, perhaps a thousand feet of it, that we had gained so painfully in the last hours. Going down hurts the legs just as much as climbing up does, and we complained a bit by way of keeping up our strength.

Coming into camp I noticed Barbara, one of the three young women in the group. She was sitting in the sun looking somewhat huddled. Her long brown hair was wet.

"Did you wash your hair?" I asked, making conversation.

"I fell in an ice pool," she said, in her quiet way.

I gawked at her, not comprehending, and was told by one of the others of Barbara's near death. It seems one of the porters had slipped down a rocky pitch on the glacier and had fallen into one of the barely melted pools that the sun had formed out of the glacier during the day. Barbara was near him when he fell, and seeing that he could not climb out, reached to give him a hand. She fell in, too, and found to her horror that not only was her heavy pack pulling her down, but there was no bottom to the pool to push off from, nor handhold on the edge of the pool to grasp. Only loose rocks and near freezing water. One could live only a few minutes in such a pool, and if there had not been a couple of other people nearby at that moment, both Barbara and the porter would have died.

63

This story was a confirmation of the feeling of abandonment we had when there was no one in sight. For one reason or another, it frequently happened that one was alone or with only one other in all that treacherous country. The anxiety of being human in an inhuman setting was joined with the fear of physical dangers, and Barbara's experience gave substance to our constant worry. One could die here, with no resources beyond one's own. Apart from the psychic disturbance created by invading forbidden territory, it was becoming clearer and clearer that we were having to discover ever deeper levels of ourselves in order to survive at all.

One could not always see in time what the dangers were and even when they were visible, it was often necessary to proceed right into them; and this required an expectation that the necessary strength and agility would be there as needed. There was no way of testing one's capability in advance. You had to jump into the situation, whatever it was, and gradually realize that you can do more than you can do. It was a hard time, and there was much ahead that had no shape as yet.

Shape came to our experiences only in retrospect.

XIII

The avalanche came down like a thunder roll and fetched up at the bottom with a heavy th-*wump.*

I came awake at once, eyes wide open and not understanding. Then I saw the white cloud rising from the bottom of the ravine splitting the mountain wall directly opposite, and knew it was an avalanche.

It was night and except for the replays of the avalanche in my mind, all was quiet. It was dark yet not dark, because of the stars. At this altitude they were like light bulbs, big and illuminating. Even as there was little atmosphere to mediate the hot sun, so there was little to dim the starlight. I could read my watch. Twelve-thirty.

I sighed. I had slept about four hours and knew that I would be awake the rest of the night. The primarily carbohydrate diet resulted in a sugar drop that woke me after only a few hours' sleep each night. But this particular camp was extra painful. Klaus and I had spent a long time the evening before trying to arrange the rocks so they presented as smooth a surface as possible. We had foam pads, but their one-inch thickness could not absorb such rocky irregularities. Now I could feel a chart on my back of the individual shape of each rock.

I squeezed my eyes tight and willed sleep. Then I turned and tried to make a place for my hip so I could lie on my side. Then my stomach. And finally on my back again. All useless. Furthermore the icy night wind kept whistling down my neck. I tried to adjust my parka to block it. Except for my boots, I was fully dressed in my sleeping bag, which made tossing and turning difficult.

Frank had said there were satellites passing overhead that were visible at night so I entertained myself for a while looking for them. Apparently Frank slept indifferently, too. I wondered how many others were lying awake in the camp. Klaus, beside me, was snoring softly, but I knew he would not sleep all night either, and that I would have his company soon.

Really, the nights were long. Also uncomfortable. But I was getting the rhythm of them and used to waiting. In time it would be dawn, and the cooks would begin breakfast preparations.

And so it was. By five-thirty the camp was awake and busy. There was a different atmosphere today because it had been decided we would have a rest day. That would give the sick ones a chance to catch up on their health, and the others a chance to explore the view.

Standing up by the cooking area, eating cereal out of my cup, I heard a shout from a distance. There, trotting along, came Jock and the cook Hussein! We watched them come briskly down the track we had struggled over the day before. Here it was not even eight o'clock in the morning and they had already made the trip that took us nearly nine hours the day before. The difference in mountaineering experience was once again brought home to us.

It turned out that it had taken them only four hours of marching to catch up to us. Of course, they had escaped the sun's havoc this way, and did all their climbing in the cool. But the fact remained that they knew their business, and we were impressed.

Jock came noisily into camp full of excitement about the terrain and scenery, and immediately began arranging with a porter to carry his photography gear up into the mountains for a picture-taking climb. Exploring new mountains and taking pictures were his greatest joys, and it was a pleasure to watch him emerge from his customary negativity and sourness.

Klaus and I debated making a climb to get a view of the whole range. His feet were very bad, and his spirits were low. However, he decided to give it a try.

As for me, I discovered something. In spite of my continuing state of anxiety and exhaustion, I realized that I had indeed chosen

66

this trip. The negative attitude I had had was as one-sided as Jock's, which may have been why I resented him so much. Whether it was the surprise of seeing him happily anticipating his day that brought about my own attitude change, or whether I came up with it myself is unclear. The fact was that I was enthusiastic about exploring without schedule or having to get anywhere.

Our setting was extraordinary. The camp in the river bed was about a thousand feet below the pass. Here the scene had changed from being in a bucket, as it was below at Shotaling, to being in a large bowl. We were just down from the lip of the bowl on the western side. Like the round sides of the bowl extending in a great circle out from us, the mountains ringed around the glacier that fell away below us.

Rising softly in the middle of the bowl at the head of the glacier was the large round hill of grass, streams, and flowers that we had traversed the day before. Its base was just a few yards from our camp. It looked as though, were one to climb up on top of this great mound, it would be possible to get a three-hundred-sixty degree panorama of all the mountains in this area.

With packs containing food, water, and cameras, and carrying an ice axe and umbrella respectively, Klaus and I began to ascend the green hill.

It had been a deceptive scene. The apparent hill was actually a vertical ascent. One had to climb it sideways, either traversing, switching back and traversing the opposite way in a zigzag, or else sidestepping straight up it. Either way, very hard on the feet, and about three hundred feet up, Klaus decided to go back. His loafers were just no good for this kind of climbing and there were at least another five or six hundred feet to the top of the hill.

Feeling the strength of my choice, I indicated regret for his situation and my intention to continue alone. Others had gone ahead, and looking down I could see that more were coming along, but there was so much sheer space everywhere that I truly felt on my own. I watched Klaus begin to pick his way down the hill, then turned to continue climbing. It was very hard work. The altitude was fifteen or sixteen thousand feet, the sky was cloudless and the sun, pure heat.

But with my attitude of choice came extra strength, and even my umbrella seemed to catch an updraft to help lift me on my way.

More and more I was experiencing separateness. Each day I realized more sharply that I alone inhabited my body, lifted my feet, leaned forward into the hill to ease the drag of my rucksack. I alone arranged to breathe in a rhythm of in, then in some more, then slowly out, timing my rhythm to my steps. There was comfort in the intake of air and the soft rush of exhaling.

Then there was the slim handle of my umbrella that provided my balance. I could see why a tightrope walker uses an umbrella; it is indeed an instrument of balance. Furthermore it was beginning to carry a magic feeling for me of making possible a daily contact with the sun. The Icarus problem of flying too high was very real here, in this experiment in *hubris*. The wax that held my wings together was in constant danger of melting and there was something about my umbrella that placated the gods.

It is only now, in remembering, that I recognize these things. On that day, daring to climb for a view of these mountains, I knew only a vague prickling of anxiety and excitement, a vague unease and hurry that kept me moving. Mainly I thought little, just was my body, step, lift, bring up the other foot, step, lift, bring up the other foot. Mindless, all was body.

And then I was up. Straight down, a thousand feet below, lay the camp by the great rock in the dry part of the river bed. It would have been so easy to pitch forward and fall to the bottom. I almost wanted to do it.

Pulling on consciousness I turned to look where I had climbed to. Now I could see that the top of the hill was in fact the lower edge of a long gentle rise up to a rocky promontory which would indeed permit a total panorama. I marched on up this slope. I could climb directly now, and it was an enjoyable experience. I was walking on a short tough green of low-lying grasses, strewn everywhere with flowers of many colors. And again, here were the pale blue butterflies. A breeze cooled the scene and I felt utterly charmed. Here was the small, the single flower, the fluttering butterfly. Here was singleness and warmth. I could touch this and that; I felt my humanness. Only then did I begin to know what was lost in the awesome scenes we had come through. The mountains shocked me in their monstrous impersonality. I was without a name there. But with grass underfoot and flowers all around I was again in the picture, and the effect was magical.

At last I arrived at the promontory. Two or three others had already found seats there and I joined them. No one said much. But it was nice to be in their company, because here I had to receive again the heavy impact of the great mountains encircling us.

From this perch of perhaps fifteen thousand feet, high on the great mound that rose up in the middle of the mountain bowl, I looked up and around. Six and eight thousand feet above me they rose, looking back down at me, tiny pimple on a hill. Forbidding, black and white they circled me, sharp and stark against the sky.

I could not think about the scene then; I was owned by it, I, the least part of it. But apparently I recorded the whole of it in me somewhere, because it is instantly available in my mind's eye. It moves me still, I think it always will, the picture and knowledge of raw power that held me clamped to my place on that promontory. Even to be in the picture, even as least part, was to be charged with awe and privilege.

The author, halfway up Aghost Bar glacier, looking
back down to Shotaling

Photo Frank Fitzgerald

XIV

Today we would climb to the top of the Thui An Pass, and the breakfast atmosphere was charged. I stood with the others, feeling thrilled by the prospect of that climb. Though the top of the pass was not much higher than the hill I had climbed the day before, the significance of it was undeniable. I anticipated experiencing mastery of something, of standing in substantial relation to those fierce mountains, and of completion. After the pass would come a descent into new territory and new negotiations with the unknown.

Looking up to the pass from camp I saw the smooth rise of loose rock lying at the angle of repose. Up it sloped, about a thousand feet above us, and I was glad we had started extra early this morning. The sun would not rise above the eastern wall of mountains for two or three more hours, and I did not mind the briskness of the morning air. We might get well up on that great slope of scree before the heat began.

From the hill yesterday I had studied the pass and had observed the faint trace of a track angling across and up the scree. Apparently, goats travelled across this pass and had developed a slim path. This was the track we would take since it would provide a base of sorts, such that our weight would not dislodge the lightly poised rocks.

It was a steep angle to climb at this altitude, but then that meant fewer steps. I was anxious nonetheless, partly because of the physical demand of the pass, but also because of the forbidding look of this largest of all stony dunes. Bleak, dark grey slate unrelieved by any color or life. Also I was afraid the rocks would be alive underfoot, requiring the kind of effort dune-climbing does, of two steps forward and one step back and the wild churning of feet required for even that much result. Or worse, a terrible sidewise slide to the bottom.

Klaus and I met Frank and Tom to pair up for the climb. I attached myself once again to Frank's boots, while Klaus took position behind Tom in order to herd him along, and we set off. A group of porters were just ahead of us, and we let them lead us.

Leaving the camp, we went up the river bed for a while, until we came to a great snow bridge that took us west across the river. It felt quite solid and we crossed easily, only to be greeted by a steep incline of untracked scree. The path was above us, and to get to it required a tough scramble up through rolling, sliding rocks. All of us and the porters fought for footing and each was on his own here. It was important not to get behind any of the others because of the rocks flying from their boots. So each picked his own way, and it was a hectic scene of puffing and stumbling and scrambling feet.

My edema bothered me some. It had steadily worsened, though it seemed that I still was not in too much danger from it. I was coughing at intervals of twenty or thirty minutes day and night, but in the daytime this was just one more phenomenon of being in these high places. At night the coughing was a problem. The sessions were more frequent when I was horizontal and they woke me up. I learned to prop myself up so that I lay at a slope rather than flat, and that helped.

The main difficulty of the present fight to gain altitude in the scree was that my swollen legs and feet were less agile than usual. Also, I was inhibited in using my arms and hands to clutch and prop me up, since the tight skin stretched over the swollen tissues felt as though it might pop like sausage casing. I was reminded briefly of my pregnancies years ago, and my anxious slathering on of lotion to lubricate the skin on my belly so that it would be flexible enough to stretch over the growing baby without splitting open.

Even at that time I realized what a ludicrous concern this was, but my judgment was perhaps a bit off its usual base. At sixteen thousand feet the oxygen is thin; the other physical conditions of fatigue, sun and heat exhaustion, and dehydration must all have an effect on normal perceptions.

When at last I stood on the goat path, I was dizzy and panting, like an exhausted animal. While trying to recover my equilibrium, I looked down the slope we had just climbed and was impressed. From here looking down it seemed unlikely that we could have kept our footing well enough to get up. Furthermore, there was no sign of our passage. The scree was again lying at the angle of repose, no tracks, no steps visible.

Perhaps two hundred feet below us was the great rock around which the camp had been set up. Dwarfed now by the vast scenery surrounding it, the rock looked at odds with the great upthrusts of mountain peaks. It seemed to be a huge block chiselled and ready to be put in place in a pharoah's pyramid. Out of place in this ruthless scenery.

Frank said, "Shall we go on?" and I recognized the urgency of getting as far as possible before the sun hit. I turned and plugged into his heels as he started off up the narrow strip of goat track. The footing was better now; the goats had packed the rock with their tough little feet.

Tilting as far forward as I could without falling, I tried to center my gravity enough off-balance for my feet to be compelled to keep moving. It was an uncomfortable posture, bent forward that way, with my backpack adding its full weight, but it served the purpose of keeping my feet moving.

My mind faded, my world became narrowed down to Frank's boot rising, revealing a footprint into which my boot went. A rhythm began of step, breathe in, step, breathe out, and that was enough for a while.

Then the sun burst on us, like a hot flood, and conditions worsened immediately. My rhythm became agitated: step, breathe in, breathe out, step, breathe in, breathe out, the sequence was too fast for comfort. I began to feel panicky; I couldn't get the oxygen in fast enough, I felt strangulated. As the panic built, the sense of suffocation increased.

Suddenly Frank stopped and I nearly ran into him.

"We'll stop a minute," he said calmly.

My hysterical breathing soon quieted, as we stood there, and Frank grinned.

"Slow and easy," he stated and started to move again.

My panic receded; I knew Frank had heard what was happening, and that I could rely on him to handle the situation. We would step, breathe, step, breathe, in a slow, deliberate way for perhaps fifteen minutes, stop for two or three minutes, then proceed again. The track up the bony flanks of Thui An Pass was steep, but the rate of rise was regular, and it was possible to maintain the rhythm all the way up. I saw nothing but Frank's boots, and the black-grey slope they were traversing. On and on, up and up.

When a strong cold wind caught me in the face I came suddenly to consciousness. It was with a jolt that I realized we had arrived at the top of the pass. We were all the way up. Never before had I experienced being all the way up, in just that sense. I stood on the top of Thui An Pass and exulted. Above me was sky, free of peaks and overhang. Now the peaks were in front of me, behind me, but I no longer experienced them as above me.

What must it be like to stand on top of such peaks? I truly cannot conceive of that. It was sufficient for me to stand where I was. All the way up. Sixteen thousand feet above sea level, and at least five or six thousand feet above the lower edge of the huge Thui An glacier, which I could see in its entirety. The vast bowl with its ring of mountains and its bottom scoured by the great glacier lay before me. The peaks were all another five to ten thousand feet higher than our vantage point, but that detracted not at all from my feeling that I was all the way up. Now I had deep pleasure in the scene, free of the cringing fear that something would topple over and crush me.

It was bitterly cold on the sharp edge of the ridge that was Thui An Pass connecting two mountains. The wind blew right through the space between the mountains, honing the pass into a razor edge. We sat just below the edge, out of the worst of the wind and relished our arrival.

We laughed when two white birds the size of pigeons flew just over our heads. They came from the far side of the pass and flew on

74

down the slope we had just climbed. This was the first animal life we had seen since the goats invaded our camp several days before, and the obvious symbolism embarrassed us. Perhaps it was a group hallucination, a creation of something we needed to have appear, but I am convinced those birds were real.

And there we sat or lay back against the black rocks, facing the sun and the glacier we had climbed. We were glad now for the heat to combat the snow-chilled wind. We drank our grey glacier water, noting the gritty residue in our teeth, not caring in the least. Someone passed around some hard candy; someone else had peanuts and we were entirely pleased with the world.

The author negotiating the Aghost Bar glacier
leading up to Thui An Pass

XV

While we were sitting there, glorying in our mastery of Thui An Pass, monsoon clouds were bunching up overhead. They were rolling in from the southwest behind us, black and wild, carried along by the cold wind. Our climbing satisfaction was great enough to block awareness of the collapsing weather, however. It was not until the great couloir of snow in front of us that was the west face of Thui An Mountain suddenly became shadowed over that we looked up to discover the rain clouds overhead.

We scrambled up, gathering ourselves for the next stage of our expedition, the descent down the other side of the pass to the Gazin glacier a thousand feet below. For all that we had surmounted this first long haul, we were still in the middle of our day's journey, and we had much yet to do.

Standing in the by now forceful, bitter wind on the ridge top, we surveyed the next stage. Falling several hundred feet down and away from us was a scree slope like the one we had just come up. A narrow goat path made its way at the steepest possible angle. But Jock, in his usual aggressive manner, directed us to take the slope straight down in a sliding run, very much as one might descend a sand dune.

"Be sure you take your weight on your thighs," he boomed, "or you'll get what they call around here, Sahib's knee." He laughed; he did not care much what we did.

The fact is, no matter how many sand dunes you have run or slid down, the first time down a slope of loose rock is an adventure! Before I could think about it too much, I took off. On the same premise as in skiing, that it is essential to lean away from the hill so as to keep your feet under you, I virtually fell forward down the slope.

It worked pretty well, especially after I established a rhythm. Step, slide, step, slide, knees bent, weight on my thighs, gravity working for me, for a change. Whooping, I "skied" down the hill. Perhaps I was a bit drunk in the thin air and the first real descent in the whole trip thus far.

Later we learned that the elegant Jahangir had raced someone else down the mountain, had fallen, somersaulted several times, and landed at the bottom with what may have been cracked ribs. So the booby traps were still there, even though there was the reprieve from climbing.

Below the scree slope was a chaotic tumble of gigantic boulders, extending several hundred more feet down. This rockfall was full of more or less vigorous streams of water, bubbling and falling to a small plain beyond. The trick was to pick your way through these great rocks without having to traverse too many of the waterfalls. Yet it was often necessary to move across the rockfall and the streams to discover another downward route. We all fell in, at one time or another, for the rocks were slippery and unstable. Klaus and Tom were particularly liable with their loafers and tennis shoes.

My knees began to go. All our marching until now had been upward; on this, our first long descent, we discovered new weaknesses. Unused muscles, lax tendons around joints, uncalloused skin. I became anxious about dropping down from one rock to the next, for fear that a knee would give way and I would fall onto the rocks. It was an alarming prospect, to fall here. Since the boulders were huge, the drops were great, and there were some vicious projections and edges. Or it was possible to fall into narrow crevices between boulders, perhaps breaking bones in the process.

Fatigue accelerated with fear, now an added ingredient. Descending the great jumble of boulders seemed to take forever. My knees trembled constantly, and I had to keep sitting down to take my weight off of them. The flat below seemed to remain at the same distance, and the rains were threatening to begin any minute. When they came we knew that the slipperiness would be increased, so we felt the pressure of time. Often we would have to retrace our route back from a dead end; as usual, we were left to our own devices to find our way through the rock labyrinth. Worse, we saw no signs of the camp, though porters had gone ahead. Perhaps the camp was not on this flat area, after all, and we would once more find that the day's march was half again as long as we thought.

We were not talking now, having to focus utterly on our footing, not daring to look around for fear of misstepping. Again the experience of mindlessness with everything oriented around legs and feet. Drops of rain began to fall, but mercifully the rocks began to be more widely spaced, footing improved, even sections of goat track became visible. We had navigated the great rockfall and were now on the plain.

Two small boys materialized in front of us, bringing us out of the isolation we each had been in. Good-looking children, but old somehow. One knew a few words of English, incredibly, though very difficult to understand.

"Third grade," he said proudly. "Learn English."

We smiled at them, while Frank tried to make conversation. It was a bit unrewarding, the conversation, but much warmth and amiability was exchanged all around. Frank gave them each hard candy; we all shook hands, and the boys guided us to our camp. It had been set up behind a low rise in the center of the plain, which is why we had not been able to see it.

In preparation for the monsoon storm a cook tent had been set up for the first time. The provisions and stores, along with the cooks, nearly filled the space under the tent, so we all huddled around the outside in the fairly strong rain. Ray parcelled out sleeping tents; Klaus and I began to try to figure ours out. Though he had years ago been in the business of manufacturing camping equipment, and we had, as a young family, done some overnight trips into the Sierra foothills, both of us found modern gear a mystery. Ray came by, saw us entangled in ropes and canvas, and without comment pitched in to help us.

The prospect of a tent enchanted me. An enclosure. For all this time I had been in the open, subject to the incursions of mountain

79

archetypes and the glances of others. The effort to shield myself, maintain a psychic privacy, was largely unconscious, but now that there was an opportunity to let the tent shield me, I could feel the strain I had been carrying all along. The monsoon was, after all, a blessing. As soon as the tent was up, I crawled inside, and tight though the quarters were, I wallowed in the feeling of being contained.

Klaus came inside, too, but was somewhat less delighted with the situation. By the time our two sleeping bags were spread out, our duffles arranged so as not to touch the tent sides, and we were both inside, there was not an inch to spare. He, being of a more extraverted nature than I, rumbled something about claustrophobia, and extricated himself to go back outside. I got up only for dinner, waiting until the last minute, listening to the rain fall on the tent and the wind tug at its pegs.

When I went out, I really looked at the scenery for the first time. It was entirely different from what we had been living in for so many days. We were down about a thousand feet from the pass, on a flat plain with a violent rain-fat river tearing through its center. The main source of the river was a series of glaciers lodged between each mountain and its neighbor, half-circled around us. We were again under the threat of the mountain peaks. They leaned over us as in the other valley, but here all was dark and frozen. Even on a clear day the sun did not strike these mountains, as they were all on the south side of the plain, offering their northern faces to our view. Glaciers were packed between mountains like food stuck between adjacent teeth. The run-off from these glaciers gathered into the river racing past us, and with the addition of the extraordinary rains of monsoon season, the river was in flood.

We all talked of what might happen if the rains kept on, what might happen to our present campsite; and what about the trip ahead of us: would there be an increased problem with washed-out bridges and tracks? To all of these worries Jock responded with enthusiastic confirmation of certain fearsome problems and disasters.

I went back into the tent. Jock's talk worried me, but Klaus and I were beginning to develop a plan of our own. Along with Frank and Tom, we had begun to discuss how we might be able to split off by ourselves and cut the trip shorter by heading down the present valley south to Chitral. From there we could fly out of the Himalayas. The expedition's planned route was to turn back up north to another pass and over into a third valley.

I knew I could not survive another pass. I had to get off, and my apprehensions had been echoed by the three men. So, as I lay in the tent, I tried to calm the anxiety Jock had stirred up, cling to the hope of a new plan, and enjoy the seclusion and warm dry coziness of the tent.

Outside the storm increased its frenzy.

A porter at Thui An Pass, with Thui An Mountain
in the background

XVI

All night the rain poured down on us and the wind tore at our light tent. We lay rigidly on our backs staring into the pitch darkness, expecting at any moment to be carried away like a package. Since the floor of the tent was sewn to its sides, the weight of our bodies provided an anchor against the storm, but we did wonder if our weight was sufficient, or whether the top of the tent might be ripped away leaving us exposed. Avalanches were being released by the rain-soaked glaciers all around the camp, sounding as if they would roll right over us. We were in the vortex of forces beyond knowing, a vast, wild whirlpool of chaotic energies.

At last, toward dawn, the monsoon lessened; and we dozed lightly until the cooks started banging around. Their voices were full of complaint as they struggled with muddy equipment and wet food. We crawled out of our tent, blinking and battered, to take stock of our situation.

The first sight that caught our attention was the river running so high that it seemed to mound up above its banks. Still, though it heaved along in great waves and eddies, it did not flood over into our campsite. Perhaps the downhill slope was sufficiently steep to compel the water to fall forward rather than spread out to the sides. The effect was alarming, nonetheless, as it ran past us, humped like the back of a great, grey serpent.

Breakfast was soggier than usual, but it served the purpose of providing a time of gathering round and developing momentum for the day. We stood in damp misery, warming our hands on the hot teacups, as the waning monsoon dropped its soft rain on us. The most miserable factor was the heavy fog that draped us totally. The whole plain was white with it, down to the ground, and visibility was reduced to a few yards.

Everything dripped, soaked through, and in spite of our parkas, we soon progressed from damp to wet, too. We dismantled our tents with cold fingers, barking our knuckles on pegs and metal fittings. Complaining and inefficient, we packed ourselves up for the next glacier, obscured in the fog, but inescapably in our path.

Beth and Michael, two of the younger people, led off. They were increasingly a couple, and stayed close together on the marches. Young Charles followed, with me on his heels and Klaus behind me. We plunged into the fog, starting off bravely enough on a definite path.

It soon disappeared into the rocks and ice of the glacier. Actually, this glacier was principally moraine. Most of the snow and ice had receded, and we were confronted by another great mass of heaped and tumbled rocks and boulders. As on the other glacier, there was no path, but our progress was impeded even more here by the white-out of the fog and rain. It was impossible to pick out a route more than a step or two in advance. It was not even possible always to tell which way was downhill, given the confusing visibility and heaps of moraine that required as much climbing as descending. I fixed my attention on Charles's feet. For all his youth, there was a sureness about him in this difficult terrain that I trusted. As we went along I realized that I was letting him absolutely guide me. Sometimes Michael and Beth would disappear in the fog, but I held my connection with Charles.

After a while I realized Klaus was no longer behind me—just Charles, scrambling and jumping rocks in front of me. I put my worry for Klaus aside and followed Charles grimly. If I lost him now, I would be left to my own inadequate resources. It was very difficult to keep up with him, but survival required it, so I extended myself utterly to take the long leaps and brave risks Charles was making ahead of me. And, to my amazement, not one rock rolled under our feet, not one dead end closed our way, not one slip resulted from the rain-slick. On and on Charles plunged, never resting his weight on one foot, always moving on to the next step and the next.

After about an hour we came out of the moraine, though the visibility was as short as before. The rain still came gently, inexorably down; everything we wore and carried was wet through, and the fog was a shroud. But good earth was underfoot, and sometimes a path. It was a lovely feeling to put my boot down on flat surface again. We seemed to be crossing a meadowlike place, now, and I could see Michael and Beth stopped ahead of us. We caught up to them, and stood for a few minutes, fishing out hard candies, and talking a little. The great exertion and jogging of the past hour had left me comfortably warm, and somewhat to my surprise, I was not especially winded or tired.

But when we fell silent, I experienced again the awe of my surroundings. Here we were, a little cluster of four, and all around us, hidden in the mist and fog, was the alien land that neither knew our language, nor cared for our lives. If we disappeared into the obscurity, it would be as if we had never been. My own reality seemed in question. The others seemed to feel it, too. Turning, they started off again without further talk.

They were really too fast for me, but the alternative of being left alone in this invisible place was enough of a spur to keep me with them. Finally, I realized that I had just to let myself go, to fall forward down the mountain, letting my feet find footing as necessary. And even without being able to see ahead, the attitude worked. Without really seeing where I was putting my feet, just keeping my eyes fixed on Charles's running boots, I was all right.

Then Beth and Michael stopped suddenly. The path had completely vanished. I stood quietly, waiting for them and Charles to find the way, realizing how totally I had placed myself in their hands. It was strange to relinquish my autonomy so completely, but comfortable. I knew they would find the way, and they did. All three of them were highly experienced hikers and climbers, and seemed to know how to pick up a lost track. Soon we were running again. Not since I was a child had I run for so long. Yet in the cool of the light rain, falling with gravity down the mountain, I felt as though I could go on indefinitely.

But now, we came to a river. Roaring and plunging, it came torrentially down the slope. It was overflowing its banks, and we saw that the footbridge had been swept away.

"Come on!" shouted Charles, leaping from rock to rock through the swollen river. Without stopping to think, I threw myself after him. In the moment between his jumps and mine, the river rose several inches, so that the rocks I jumped to were already underwater by the time I landed on them. I just kept going and my forward momentum carried me across.

The others also crossed haphazardly, but safely, and we looked back. The river was rising and rising, just as we looked, and now it would require plunging through its depths to cross. No stepping rocks were visible any more. I worried about Klaus, but put the thought aside as the others took off again.

I followed them through the fog and down the mountain for a long time more, crossing another flooded river safely. Then we came to the edge of what must have been the principal river of the whole valley. Huge and brown, it tore at its banks, swirling great boulders and debris along with it. We were above it, traversing the rocky cliff that sloped steeply to it. The narrow track we were on was loosening, and the rocks that were the cliff were beginning to move. The great quantities of rain falling began to drive the rocks down the slope like a monstrous avalanche, and our track began also to slip inexorably toward the river.

There was only one thing to do and that was to increase our speed and try to stay ahead of the collapse of the rock slopes. We raced and scrambled, often on hands and knees, shouting encouragement to each other. Our frantic pace took us across slope after slope of the heavy, sliding, water-laden rocks, until at one point we were stumbling through ankle-deep waves at the edge of the river.

Fast, fast, we ran pell-mell along the river until suddenly an irrigation ditch angled off to the side. Gratefully we veered off to run on its muddy but sound banks until we were safely away from the river. Then, gasping and horrified, we stopped and stared at each other, deeply aware of how near we had come to being taken away by the river, and ground to bits among its rolling boulders.

A quick alarm over Klaus insisted on rising through me. I felt great fear for him; if things were so bad when we came through, what would he face coming after?

Subdued, we made our way slowly to the muddy hut where Jahangir and Saïd had already arrived and were waiting anxiously for us.

Jahangir, facing camera, negotiates with porters.

XVII

Standing on the porch of the hut, I peered into the lightening fog and drizzle, trying to see if Klaus was coming. It was no longer possible to hold at bay the worry I felt about him. Especially as others of the group and several porters arrived, dripping wet, but no Klaus.

We spread our outer gear around on the porch railings, on the inevitable apricot trees, but nothing could possibly dry until the sun reappeared. Crowded together in the minimum shelter of the small porch and fruit trees, we were a dismal lot.

Things improved slightly after we had eaten lunch, the usual fare of pemmican, crackers and peanuts. Added today was some canned cheese and one lovely can of sardines. We each got a tiny taste, and some also managed to pour a little of the oil onto crackers. How tired we were of our tedious diet.

But mainly I was waiting for Klaus. The possibility that he might have been hurt in the aftermath of the monsoon was pressing on me. In this moment I knew strongly the depth of the interlock that had developed between us over twenty-six years of marriage. Perhaps it was not ridiculous that I felt he would be in better circumstances were I with him.

At last, he arrived. Wet and tired, of course, but something more. A look in his eyes of shock.

Later he told me what had happened to him.

He had watched me disappear into the mists with the three young people, as he clambered more slowly through the rough moraine. He was overtaken by Ken, Charles's father, and for quite a while they proceeded together. But when they cleared the moraine Ken seemed to be anxious to move faster, so Klaus sent him ahead.

Through the meadow, and picking his way carefully along through the intricacies of the downhill track, Klaus managed well. Even crossing the greatly swollen river was all right, once he reconciled himself to sodden loafers.

The trouble came, as it did with us, in the traversing of the great loose rock slopes that followed. By this time, the avalanching action of the water had caused great vertical ravines to form, and the track had vanished. Vertical ridges remained still stable, alternating with the ravines down which avalanches rolled.

By headlong charges he was able to fall and stumble across the downward sliding ravines, until it happened that the ridge he was standing on began to roll, too. He had a moment of utter panic when he realized that all footing was now gone, that the whole rock mountain was grinding ever faster down to the river and was carrying him with it.

Suddenly out of the mists appeared one of the porters, tiny and wiry, his dark little face jutted forward. And his hand. Reaching far, far across the sliding rock, Klaus thrust out his hand to the porter. Incredibly they grasped hands, and with a great heave, the tiny man of perhaps one hundred pounds hauled Klaus, twice as heavy, to the relative safety of the porter's footing. A few minutes later, Klaus and the porter arrived at the rest hut, and except for the residual look of surprise in Klaus's eyes, he was fine.

But again, the immediacy of death was forcibly recognized, and we found we had little to say once the story was told.

We were now in the village of Gazin, and our first feeling was of having landed after a flight to somewhere unearthly. All was exceedingly strange here, but at least there were other humans, animals, cornfields, apricot trees. It was even all right to be stared at again, which we were.

Perhaps because we were among the oldest members of the group, we were assigned the porch of another rest hut for our overnight accommodations. The others would sleep in the apricot orchard. No one even suggested moving into the interior of the hut, forbiddingly dark and dank. I found myself populating it with obscure and frightening insect and reptile life. And the smell was discouraging.

Since our overnight site was a considerable hike away, we prevailed upon one of the gawking youngsters to carry our duffles for us. I was apprehensive about such a small boy carrying two twenty-five pound duffles, but he grabbed them unhesitatingly and led us to our hut.

A huge river of grey mud and water was rolling right through the village. Along its sides, where it had receded slightly with the cessation of rain, we could see remnants of broken trees, thorn fences, mud huts. Apparently the river of mud had been another great avalanche loosened by the rain, and it had swept everything away before it. The boy seemed unconcerned, as if it were a frequent occurrence, and indeed it was, we later learned. We looked for a narrow place to cross. There was none, but we did find a place where we could jump into a relatively shallow part of the river.

Klaus jumped and his feet disappeared into grey muck to the ankles. With difficulty he pulled out his feet, rescuing his wretched loafers with a sucking noise. The boy jumped, his plastic shoes also sinking deep, and there was no alternative but for me to follow.

The muck continued on the other, lower side, and we slipped and sank and slurped our way over to the hut, many yards away. It was an awful mess, and I began to wonder just how altruistic our assignment to the accommodations had been.

A spring near the main river was pointed out to us, and we managed to clean ourselves up a little, but not much. It was a good thing we had relinquished our city attitudes so thoroughly now, because there was nothing to be done about the situation.

After some debate we decided we would make our way back to the others for dinner, and we were startled to see how rapidly the washout river was receding. The incredible speed of changes in this country was again apparent. How abruptly things went from one extreme to another! This time we were able to find a narrow, muddy place to cross the river without having to jump into the water again.

We were glad we had decided to join the others when we saw

that they had made a fire. It was the first one we had seen in the Himalayas, and it was a warm sight in the still very wet apricot orchard.

Because the Himalayas are so new, geologically, there are few trees. For that matter, we saw few shrubs or plants, and rarely any dirt or natural animal life. Goats, donkeys, and a few scrawny chickens were all brought in from the lower mountains. All growth was developed by the villagers along the rivers and irrigation ditches; none of it was indigenous to these heights.

The absence of trees and shrubs meant an absence of firewood, thus a fire was a rare luxury. The one natural growth, sparsely located, that was used for fencing and tiny cooking fires was the thornbush. Tiny twigs would be carefully broken off and heaped for burning, and one piece at a time would be added to maintain the fire. Great care was needed in handling this bush since its thorns were long and wicked. So we were indeed privileged by this fire, built purely for our pleasure, for we had primus stoves for cooking.

The time had come now to gather with Frank and Tom and decide what we wanted to do about leaving the group. Gazin was at the head of a valley that dropped about six thousand feet to Chitral, perhaps a hundred and thirty miles away, where there was an airstrip. It was also the point from which the group was scheduled to go even deeper into the Hindu Kush range in the opposite direction from Chitral. The route was over yet another pass, the Shah Janali, down into the next valley, and then on into Chitral.

Even if the storm had not washed out any of the track or bridges on their route, this next pass would be higher than the one we had just crossed, and at least five days or a week would be needed to arrive at a point in the next valley analogous to where we were now in this valley. If we headed down from here we would shorten our trip appreciably and reduce the number of chances of being blocked by washouts.

We four quickly came to a consensus. We had all had enough, even Frank, who was thin but otherwise in good shape. I had the impression that he relished the idea of us going off by ourselves in such an unexplored area, and further, that he was concerned for our inexperience. As for Tom and Klaus, their feet were ragged and finished, and they were unhesitating in their choice to leave the group.

I was really worried about my lungs. The edema in my face and extremities was still pronounced, though we were down to perhaps thirteen thousand feet, and I was coughing all the time. I was not sure that I could survive another yet higher pass.

So we approached Jock and Ray with our plan. As we anticipated, our proposal elicited a string of doom statements from Jock, and some thoughtful nodding from Ray. A few members of the group put up some arguments against our leaving, and the two Pakistanis looked dubious.

Still, after much time and palaver the plan was made, though not without a firmly dour stance from Jock. He could not guarantee our safety; he himself had run into much difficulty with sickness and with the authorities last year when he was scouting this trip; there was not enough equipment for us to take pots and a stove with us; he could give us provisions for only six days; and so on and so forth. Catching Ray's eye, however, I knew he would do his best to provide us with what we needed.

Jahangir wrote out a letter for us to carry, to be presented to any police or other official we met. He thought that we would be all right as far as the government was concerned.

As for sickness, there was no doctor with us anyway, so what difference did it make if we continued without?

In consultation with a local villager, Jahangir drew us a sketchy map of this, the Yarkun Valley, showing several villages along the river, and circling the ones we could expect to reach at the end of each day. He said that, if all went well, we could expect to reach the town of Mastuj in three days' march, and that a jeep road from there (we could imagine what that looked like) went the remaining eighty miles or so to Chitral.

Two young boys, brothers, were hired along with their mini-donkeys, the tiniest beasts of the species I had ever seen. The boys would come early in the morning to load our gear and provisions. Feeling light with anticipation of going home, we overrode our own anxiety about this new venture. Picking our way gingerly through the now dark night back to our sleeping porch, negotiating the greatly diminished mud river, we forgot our discomfort and perpetual hunger in excited discussion of our finally leaving this so difficult country.

So relieved were we that we could only roar with laughter hours later when Klaus came awake with a horrified squawk. In the slight light of stars we saw an enormous toad galumping away as fast as it could. It had wakened Klaus by jumping on his head.

XVIII

After the toad plopped squashily away, we remained awake. I found myself feeling anxious in the deep darkness, though at first all seemed as before. Then I realized that it was raining again, and I had a sudden vision of the rivers engulfing us. The main valley river ran across the front of our hut; the mud river that was sweeping down from the mountains behind us ran alongside the hut. Since I could see nothing at all, I strained to hear what was happening. Both rivers were roaring, and it occurred to me that we might become cut off from the others if the washout between us increased in size. Furthermore, what did continued monsoon rains mean to the river valley ahead of us? Would the track be erased, bridges washed away? Would we be hopelessly delayed?

I sat up quickly as I recognized the ominous roll of an avalanche. Then another. It was in front of us, across the main river. It sounded close, as if the river had risen greatly. I thought the falling slopes might swallow us up.

My scalp prickling, I spoke softly to Klaus. He was as frightened as I, not only for our proposed march down this, the Yarkun Valley, but also for our immediate safety. He had an added level of distress too, and he tried to describe it. I soon realized that he had had a complete loss of faith in our ability to extricate ourselves from these vast reaches. He had begun to despair as he listened to the awesome forces all around us.

It was as if we had awakened into a nightmare rather than out of one, and I groped for my flashlight. Its small beam was comforting in that it illuminated us to each other, though it made no dent on the darkness that was bearing down upon us.

Talking and huddled together, we waited. Finally, finally the sky lightened, and as it did, the rains let up. As we could begin to see around us, our courage returned, especially when we saw that both rivers were still safely within their banks, and that we could make it across to the others of our group. Gathering our gear, we slowly began to pick our way through the grey sludge and briskly running mud-water to join the others for breakfast.

An hour later the two brothers had loaded their tiny donkeys with our duffles as well as the stuff given us by Ray. This included a primus stove, kerosene, and several containers of dehydrated food, peanuts, cheese and crackers. Though each donkey must have weighed little more than a hundred pounds, each was loaded with eighty to one hundred pounds of provisions and equipment. Trying not to think about that too much, we headed off down the track after them.

The older brother was perhaps in his early twenties, but the younger one, who spoke a few words of English, could not have been more than twelve years old. They wore the loose cotton clothes of the Himalayas, and strange plastic oxfords (very good for slopping through mud and water). They had, as well, anomalous black pin-striped jackets, perhaps gifts from some foreigner. Both were handsome in an unfamiliar way, with finely drawn features. They were no more than five feet tall and very thin. I stared uncomprehendingly at the older one because there was something at variance in his appearance.

"Perhaps he is a descendant of Alexander the Great," said Klaus, in answer to my unspoken question. "That could account for the red hair and blue eyes."

Of course, that was it! This young man was of a coloring that jarred with the dark skin of the other people in this area. Except that, as I began to pay more attention, I saw a number of such fair individuals, startling alongside their dark fellows.

Whacking at their little donkeys with branches they pulled from nearby apricot trees, the boys marched ahead of us. I lowered my eyes to the matchstick legs of the donkeys and began to fall into a rhythm corresponding to their tiny hooves. It was comforting to be paced.

"For goodness sake!" Klaus said suddenly, and I looked up quickly to be confronted by a large field of marijuana growing in orderly rows. "It is grown as a crop here, I guess," he said, looking a bit uncertain.

"You've got to have something for comfort," I said grumpily, looking back down at the rough path. It was so easy to slip and stumble, what with the rocks, and I had probably missed all sorts of scenery because of watching my feet.

After a time we began to be overtaken by the main group, since our path did not diverge until we reached the first bridge. At that point they would proceed to the right up the valley to the next pass, and we would swing left on the other side of the river, heading down the valley.

When we came to the intersection we said goodbye to the group. As they went on, we looked at each other in some discomfort made up partly of guilt for quitting, partly anxiety for striking out unguided. Yet smug, too, for escaping what we were sure would be a hard, grinding climb. Furthermore, the sky was still massed with clouds, and it occurred to us that the rains might continue, blocking views and increasing the dangers to be faced by the others.

At any rate, the decision was made and we headed off on our own.

The first few hours were really pleasant. With the sun subdued by clouds, the heat was less than usual. The track was reasonably plain, and mostly sloped gently downhill. It followed the river, a pleasant companion, though churning and muddy from the monsoon. At least there was some green alongside, even a few ragged trees here and there.

We stopped now and then to look at the scenery. Far back in the direction we were coming from, we had extraordinary glimpses between cloud formations of monstrous peaks and glaciers just this side of the pass. We had descended several hundred feet in the storm yesterday and could now get some feeling for where we had been.

97

Above and beyond the small village of Gazin stretched the enormous canyon back and back up to those great snow mountains. And we had just come through there the day before. We were impressed by our accomplishment.

As the morning wore on, however, the sun managed to increase its intensity between clouds and through the mist, and we began to plod. Our stops to look became fewer, our conversation dried up, and I began to think about our stopping place. According to Jahangir we should stop at Palur, about ten or twelve miles downriver from Gazin. "A short day," was the comment, as usual.

For me there was no "short day" in the Himalayas. I was always in trouble with the sun and the heat, swollen with edema yet dehydrated, always tired and hungry, and a little lightheaded in the thin air. So by two o'clock I had had it.

Luckily, Palur materialized soon. The usual village of perhaps ten mud huts, fields of puny corn, scratching skeletons of chickens, apricot trees, and staring people. Children began to hover near us as we trudged along. Women, shaking mulberry trees over great cloths to collect the fruit, stopped their work to peer at us sideways from behind their veils.

The men stared openly. Some greeted us with the now familiar "Salaam"; others remained impassive. Our donkey owners led us off the main track up a slight slope into a small courtyard of dust and donkey droppings that fronted the village Rest House. It was, as usual, a mud hut with a verandah extending along its front side. This too had a dirt surface. We heard activity within and could see that several men were sitting around on the ground of the dim interior, talking.

Gratefully, we sat down, too, while the boys unloaded the donkeys. We unrolled our bedding and pulled out food for lunch. Incredibly, Frank had scrounged a can of sardines, and we all watched hungrily as he opened it up.

In seconds it was finished, all but the oil. Suddenly, surprising even myself, I reached for the can, tipped it up to my mouth and greedily drank it down.

I put the can down sheepishly and looked at the other three, who were staring at me. I felt chagrin at my behavior, embarrassed that I had failed to share the oil, but my food panic had overridden everything.

After eating, we considered our situation and surroundings. The most immediate problem was water. All we saw was the inevitable ditch, and the murkiness of what we saw flowing there encouraged Frank to go off and search for a more inviting source.

The rest of us began to realize that the other "guests" at the Rest House would have to be reckoned with. Perhaps six or eight of them drew closer and closer, one old toothless individual in particular. Tom was smoking and this old man would have a cigarette, too. And another, and another. Tom began to look resentful. He had only a few left and was unsure when or if he would find more. Finally he shook his head at the old man, and was relieved when he wandered off.

Frank reappeared, saying he had found what seemed to be a spring, so Klaus and I went off to fill our water containers. We were mildly concerned to see large, soapy bubbles on the water surface, but there seemed to be little choice. Hoping our iodine would do its job, we filled up and returned to find that someone had given us an ancient enamel plate full of very ripe apricots.

Frank pointed out the man who gave them, and we grinned thanks at him. To each other we muttered our anxiety about the cracked, split fruit. Our city attitudes had yet another level to accommodate to. Gingerly, we sampled the fruit, nodding and grinning at our audience. Oh well, with luck we would be back in civilization before we died of whatever disease we were ingesting.

Soon Frank began to organize dinner preparations. He pulled out the primus stove and tried to make it work. It would not. No matter what he did, it refused to function. After a long while, he leaned back on his heels, disgusted.

"They gave us the one that has been giving them trouble the whole time," he said in frustration, leaning over it again.

By late afternoon, there must have been fifty people in and around the courtyard. Heaven knows how the word had spread so fast, but it had, and we were on display.

99

A group of eight or ten were on the verandah with us, staring and nudging each other as Frank carried on a sign language conversation with one or two of them. Wood-framed, hemp-strung cots were set up on the verandah, and these served as chairs and perches from which the men could socialize and observe us. Called a "charpoi," each cot was covered with soft rugs and blankets, and we envied the local people their comfort. We had spread our sleeping bags in one corner of the verandah on the hard-packed dirt floor, and an unyielding mattress it was.

In the courtyard, numerous men were standing or squatting on their haunches in small groups, talking with each other in whispers, laughing and eyeing us.

We felt like zoo creatures.

One wall of the courtyard was also the wall of the neighboring mud house, and on its flat roof was seated a group of veiled women. They fluttered in their light scarves and colorful clothing, covered completely to protect them from our gaze. That they were visible at all was unusual. Perhaps the safety of their roof's height and distance from us made visibility permissible. In general, the women of the high Himalayas are secluded from view.

Still, it was impossible really to see any of them behind all the fluttering light veils, though their whole manner was highly flirtatious and provocative. The three men with me were fascinated, and actually, so was I. It was a mode of behavior that scarcely exists any more in the sexually conscious West, and it had a strange power that was disturbing.

Several of the groups, including the women, were engaging in another activity that might be analogous to our gatherings at which we eat snacks, peanuts, potato chips, in a ceremonial way. Here the snack was apricot pits. With deft hands, someone would take an apricot seed, tap it with a rock, and extricate the inner pit. These were eaten by everyone with enthusiasm and in large quantity. Only later, in connection with the "laetrile" controversy, did we learn that apricot seeds contain cyanide. In the Himalayas it seemed as though there was no problem with poisoning or cancer. In fact, the seeds may have been a vital protein supplement in their skimpy diet.

100

At any rate, it was clear that a holiday had been declared and we were the main event. It was a bit like Gulliver in Lilliput. Though each of us was literally twice as big as any one of them, their numbers, and the way they moved in groups was somewhat unnerving. We were, after all, invaders and it may have been the first time they had seen anyone from the outside, and certainly the first time an unveiled woman had come to their village.

We were tense under their scrutiny. It was like being under an onslaught of little darts, so pointed were their looks at us. We were tired beyond experience anyway, and the many eyes constantly on us finally had us frazzled.

Added to our fatigue was the frustration of Frank's not being able to make the primus stove work. He struggled and fiddled, trying this and that improvisation, but the best he could do was get a small flame with which he boiled tea. There was enough for one cup each, and while that was encouraging, it was upsetting to realize that our food supplies would be diminished by the amount that needed cooking.

The last gasp of the stove was utilized in trying to cook a mess of rice and apricots. A weird concoction, but it seemed a way to make the apricots safe to eat, as well as to season the rice.

After an interminable time, we got a glutinous mush, and hunger drove us to eat it. With that, the primus stove was retired.

By now, we also needed to retire, but until darkness came, we remained impaled by our audience. Gradually, the crowd did reduce in numbers, and by the time the sun had disappeared, we had only our verandah mates to contend with.

They prepared themselves for evening by gathering together on their charpois, turning their backs on us, and entering into a noisy, argumentative discussion. Mercifuly, the conversation seemed not to be centered on us any more, and ignored, we could prepare for sleep.

But curled up in our hard beds, we could not sleep. The loud talking went on and on into the night; then it began to rain. The verandah was open on the ends; my sleeping bag was the end one, and the rain landed full on me. Complaining and bad tempered, I wrestled my parasol into a position that at least kept the rain off my head. I gave up at last on sleep, and having given up, slept.

XIX

We headed down the path the next morning in high good spirits. Cheese and crackers for breakfast and an early start. How much simpler the packing up of gear was for only four people. We had munched on our cheese and watched our two young donkey drivers load their animals to the point of disappearing from view. It was a marvel how much they could carry, though we held our breaths against their immanent collapse as they tilted and staggered under the process. While this was going on, we grinned at our sleepy porch mates, and at the women already in their observation post on the neighboring roof. As we took pictures of each other and of the village men who wanted theirs taken, too, we were lighter of mood than we had been since the first day of marching.

We had survived twenty-four hours on our own in this forbidding country, and we were going home. It is no wonder we started off feeling so hopeful.

The fact that there were trees and greenery here helped, too. Tall poplars, fields of corn, and farther along, orchards of mulberry trees provided shade and a softer aspect.

The path ran along the river again, though now and then it would be at some distance. The valley was wider here, and there were many signs of inhabitants, huts here and there, crops, goats, even an occasional horse corralled behind thorn hedges. We had the feeling of nearing civilization, despite the alien sights that were still everywhere.

Marching along a pleasant path bordered by apricot trees and thorn hedges, we might have been in a western countryside. Then we came around a bend to see a group of women flocked below a mulberry tree. They were catching falling fruit on spread cloths, as other women scrambled around up in the tree, shaking the branches. Chittering like monkeys, their long diaphanous garments fluttering, the women in the tree were as graceful as aerialists.

Shaking the fruit loose called for daring antics up in the tree and much chatter and laughing with the women holding the cloths below. Suddenly they saw us, and an odd sight for them we must have been. Instantly, all motion and sound was stilled, veils were pulled over their faces, heads averted, and those on the ground drew back.

As we came nearer, they began to peep at us; we had glimpses of black eyes, and there were hesitant gestures from a few bold ones. Mostly, though, they remained turned away and silent, until we passed by, whereupon the chittering and giggling began again.

We came after a while to a rain-swollen cataract falling from the snow peaks behind the valley wall on our right. A bridge of sorts crossed it just before it joined the main river. A narrow footway was formed by two thin tree trunks layered over with small branches and rocks. I went across it gingerly, placing each foot carefully. It would have been very easy to step on a weak place and fall through.

The boys unloaded their donkeys and carried our gear across on their backs, trip after trip, until all of it was piled up on the other side. Then, shouting and prodding, they harangued the donkeys over the bridge. Long ears waving back and forth, noses on the ground, the little beasts moved deliberately onto the hazardous surface of branches and rocks. Their tiny hooves did not slip; they made no misstep. Each foot was placed precisely and the back feet went exactly into the spots chosen for the front feet. Steadily they made their way to the other side, and I felt my shoulders relax as they made it.

While they were being loaded up again, a small group of men came toward us, three or four in the customary pajama suits, but one wearing a uniform. We waited uneasily until they came up to us, feeling vaguely like criminals. We had heard it repeated so many times that it was illegal to be in this part of the Himalayas without army escort, that we felt somehow as if we were breaking the law.

The uniformed individual was wearing what we could see was police insignia, and he approached us purposefully. While Frank shuffled through his pockets to find Jahangir's letter, the policeman asked us something incomprehensible in Urdu. The younger donkey driver told us that the policeman wanted to know what we were doing here. Frank produced our letter and gave it to him. There followed much conversation among our donkey drivers, the policeman, and interested bystanders.

At first, the stern manner and unyielding expression on the dark face of the policeman had us cluster together for comfort and support. I felt as though I had fallen into a scene from an old movie in the exotic East, being taken for a spy, and no way to explain.

In time it became clear that there was no problem, that we were merely cause for excitement, that in fact the whole region knew we were there and our movements were being closely followed—but in curiosity, not hostility.

Finally, with much nodding and bowing, smiling and gestures of good wishes, we parted from the policeman and his entourage. Relief and amusement were our main reactions as we compared notes along the path. Apparently we had cleared the hurdle of legality, and with Jahangir's note in our possession we would be given clearance as we made our way through this district.

Again we felt satisfaction in our decision to branch off on our own, and our morale was good as we went on.

Except that, by now, some four or five hours into the morning, we were beginning to feel the sun. The last of the monsoon clouds had cleared away, and the sun was fully upon us. At the same time, the scenery was beginning to change from the relative lushness we had passed through earlier, to larger and larger, treeless, stony plains. There would be a dusty little grove of poplars here and there, but little shade under them, and they became more and more rare. We stopped for an early lunch in one of these groves, and revived a little. But when we went on again, stepping out into the full glare and heat of the brassy sun right above us, our spirits sagged. No one talked any more; even the river looked hot. It was thick with mud, and rolled and boiled along in an angry way. I did not even mind when our path would veer far away sometimes. The river was no longer any comfort.

The problem with the path veering away, however, was that it would take us over a razor-back ridge that knifed down from the valley wall across our way and into the river. The path then took us in switchback fashion up the razor ridge and zigzagged back down on its other side. The expenditure of energy on these ridges did not pay off in forward progress. Each climb was two or three hundred feet, and the footing was rubbled rock and tricky. The donkeys would lurch and heave their way up, with their drivers switching at their back feet with thin branches, then slip and slide perilously down the other side.

An endless plain of shale and loose rock would follow with little or no path marked on it. Stumbling and tired, we picked our way over a series of these. The reason they looked endless, these alien wastes, was that we could not see the periodic sunken cross-ravines that broke them up, in which there might, or might not, be a few thin trees. We were discouraged enough by now to call a halt in every grove we came to, perhaps at hour or hour and a half intervals.

Then one of the boys called out. Looking down-river, in the direction of his pointing finger, we saw a small village on the other side. Fields of corn again, a heartening array of trees, and huts. This was where we would spend the night.

"Brep! Brep!" said the boy, grinning. Oh yes, Brep was the name of the village Jahangir had suggested for our second night.

Between us and Brep extended one more glaring, rock-rubbled expanse, but Frank said, "Oh, we should be there in an hour! We should be there by three o'clock! That's not too bad."

Heartened, I agreed, and joined the others with a little more energy. Plodding over the rough rocks, feeling the hot sun through my umbrella, I conjured up images of cool shade and lying back on my sleeping bag, resting from this infernal heat and fatigue. We were down to eight or nine thousand feet now, and the air seemed not only

106

hot but heavy, to me, after the lightness of the air at fifteen thousand feet. At any rate, the prospect of stopping and sitting under trees was delicious.

Again, a shout caused me to look up from my feet. Behind us the donkeys and their drivers stopped. One of them pointed to the river. A high, frail bridge led across it, and as my eye followed it to the opposite bank, I heard myself say with despair, "Oh, no!"

The other side of the river was a sheer rock wall. The bridge landed on a tiny flat space at its base, and a narrow path began there to switchback its way up the rock wall. Up and up. Disbelieving, I looked at the awful cliff across the river and could not grasp at first that that was the only way. It had not registered with me that we would have to cross the river to reach Brep. I looked frantically down-river to see if there were not some other bridge. Nothing. This was the one we would have to take, and the path up the rock cliff, rising sheer for perhaps a thousand feet, was where we would have to climb.

The author, exhausted and unveiled, under close scrutiny by people of the village Brep

Photo Tom McKinnon

XX

Utterly discouraged and numb with exhaustion, I followed the men to the bridge, which arched thinly over the great river. I watched Klaus pick his way slowly over it, tapping lightly with his ice axe before each step. He was by far the heaviest of us all; even the donkeys weighed less. If the bridge could sustain his two hundred pounds, the rest of us could relax.

The bridge was, of course, far stronger than it looked. As usual, it was uncomfortably narrow, and when it was my turn to cross, I carefully put one foot directly in front of the other. The bridge rose and sank under me with each step. It was higher than usual, apparently to ensure that the monsoon flooded river would not wash it away; most bridges we had seen were vulnerable to washout. The construction of this one had the look of relative permanence, too; planks were laid on it rather than the usual twigs and rocks. Why it should be more essential than the other bridges was not clear to me, but it certainly seemed to be.

We watched the two boys again unload the donkeys and carry all our stuff across on their backs; again several trips were required. Then, holding our breaths, we watched them bring the donkeys across. It was quite a sight to see the tiny animals proceed without hesitation, but very slowly, to step across the swaying, bouncy bridge. They, too, put their feet in front of each other, needing no wider a walkway than we did. Their lovely little heads, with the extraordinary ears, were close to the bridge, sniffing, and looking intently for their footing. And soon we were all crowded onto the small flat landing at the base of the cliff. The boys loaded the donkeys and we began to climb.

We could see what we had to do, since the entire switchback system rose straight up from where we were standing. It helped to know what was ahead of us; so even after seven long hours of marching, we began again with renewed courage. On the other side lay Brep and rest and shade.

We went along quite well, though the donkeys had trouble clearing the wall, since the duffles hanging at their sides kept bumping against the cliff. There were a number of scary moments when one or the other donkey would bump the wall and stagger away toward the offside. But somehow, each time the little beast regained his balance and was centered on the path again.

Climbing hard we reached the top ahead of the donkeys, in less than an hour, and stopped to catch our breaths. Then, looking ahead, we saw to our crushing dismay, what we still had to do. It was not a matter only of descending the other side. Ahead of us lay a succession of ridges lying across our way to Brep. We must descend this one, then climb and descend what appeared to be three more of them. Granted, each was slightly lower than the preceding one, but in the aggregate, the prospect was devastating.

It was just this sort of unpleasant surprise that I found demoralizing. Time and again, I would think I knew what was expected of me, and would prepare myself to do that, only to find that there was more and more to do. Repeatedly, I found myself going on and on with no notion where the end was. And here it was again.

I sat down on the edge of the path, so discouraged that I could not speak. Someone sighed, and said, "Oh, my God." For a while there was silence.

Then the donkeys and their drivers came up, puffing slightly. I could not believe these two young men, in their pajama suits, pinstriped western jackets and black plastic shoes with the laces missing. They had iron endurance in their thin, small bodies.

I must have been staring at them, because the younger one suddenly smiled broadly at me, and pointing, said, "Brep! Brep!" as though it were close at hand. He was trying to encourage me, but it was a chore indeed to smile back at him.

In a few moments, the boys and their donkeys clattered off down the rocky path, and painfully, we started after them. It had been a scramble coming up this great ridge, since the rocks on the path were loose and rolling, but going down was far worse. There was constant danger of rocks turning underfoot, pitching one forward, or even over the edge. Furthermore, none of us was in good downhill condition. Almost all our efforts had been uphill until now, and our downhill muscles had not had much use. It felt to me each time I put my weight on my knees that they would crumble under me and give way. It became a project not to fall with each step.

It took longer to come down the ridge than it had to go up, but we did finally arrive at the bottom. For a few minutes it was even a relief to begin to climb up the next one. But not for long. Soon, I began to feel despair again. Each step up took what seemed to be the last of my energy. Yet there was the next and next step. The thing just went on and on.

I was groggy now, dizzy in the still full sun, and utterly dried out. I had long since finished my water, and felt a thirst panic beginning. So, when two men came swinging down the ridge toward me, I was only too quick to accept the apple one of them pulled out of his pocket. I thanked him with relief, and without concern for its being clean or peeled, bit into it frantically. I did eat around the rotten spots, but really did not care that it had travelled for a distance in some recess of the man's pajama garment.

We climbed and climbed, then slipped and crippled our way down the other side. Then again, we began to climb. I was really out of it by now, hardly knew where I was. Sometimes I half fell, half sat, and felt I had no choice but to stay there. Klaus cajolled, encouraged, got mad, but stayed with me, though his own knees were so swollen and stiff that he was in severe pain. At the time I knew that to be true, but could not react to it. I cared for nothing and no one. Sometimes I realized I was crying, but I felt no emotion. Just utterly defeated.

On one occasion we sat for a while in a small gully. A little water was flowing down it, so I filled my bottles. I could not be

111

bothered to wait to disinfect with iodine, and drank the untreated water. Then as I filled them again, this time making the effort to pour in the iodine, Klaus grunted. I followed his gaze. Above us, just to the side of the stream was a pile of what appeared to be human feces. I had taken the water from below it, drunk it untreated, and I did not care.

Still, one can do more than one can do. I had known it before, but never so sharply as in these terrible mountains. Again and again, I had reached my destination. Again and again, I had exceeded my own limits. Or what I had imagined were my limits. And so it was on this occasion.

In time, we did come to Brep. I had been going a few steps, stopping to rest, then going a few more steps, for the last couple of hours. By the time we could sit for good, the sun had gone behind the mountains, and there was a cooling breeze. I was ensconced on rugs laid on the dirt by the owner of the house in front of which we were camped. Someone had brought a plate of the familiar split apricots that had been collected from the ground.

The men soon began to gather up containers to fill at the river, flowing perhaps a quarter of a mile away. They left me to supervise the camp, and I was only too glad not to move. I watched as they started off down the path, and winced for their exhaustion and painful movements. Klaus walked with completely stiff knees and a hobble gait to try to accommodate his ruined feet.

But before they were out of sight I had my own problems. With the men gone, the women were free to come out. Suddenly I was surrounded by twenty or thirty chattering, fluttering, staring women. All ages, they clustered nearer and nearer, while I shrank into myself. An ancient shrivelled woman stuck out her finger and poked my arm. Another felt my hair. Yet another put her face right up to mine and peered into my eyes. A baby was put down, and he crawled over my legs to get into my open duffle-bag, his naked body covered with dirt and cuts. One woman pointed to a great swelling on her neck and made a piteous complaint. It was clear that as a foreigner I was perceived to know medicine. All along our route, individuals from the region had come to our expedition for medical

112

aid. There were cuts and fevers, wasting illnesses, deformities. Perhaps the most common visible ailment was goiter disorder, as evidenced by massive neck swellings. Since we all were carrying iodine crystals, we felt badly that we could not undertake the necessary program of iodization. The need was so extensive, and the absence of common language so inhibiting, we just had to smile sadly and shake our heads in helplessness when presented with the symptom. We did dispense aspirin, disinfect cuts, stick on bandaids, cluck over eye problems. But I felt bitterly the disappointment in their faces when our magic turned out to be so weak.

Enveloped in this cloud of women, feeling suffocated and crowded, I did not care about their needs; I could only try to preserve myself. It was as if they would absorb me totally, assimilate me into their ranks, and I would disappear. I was on the edge of hysteria.

Eventually the men reappeared, and the women vanished. They disappeared so quickly and silently, it was almost as if I had imagined their earlier presence. In relief, I described the experience to the men, but knew I was not conveying the deep horror I had felt. There is an archaic quality to women in these mountains, a primitive, potent flood of power that is held so totally in check in the West that it is no wonder western women have demonstrated a terrible anger in recent times. To have held in suppression such enormous forces must have developed their awesome potential of energy.

I saw it again a little later in the evening. A sudden hawing by the donkeys was followed by shouting and yelling. Our two donkeys had become tangled up in a fracas with the donkeys of our host, and suddenly a man grabbed the arm of a woman and started wrenching her around, shouting wildly at her. She, in turn, fought equally wildly, flailing at the man, jerking away, screaming. Without even quite understanding what the fight was about, I was struck by the utter equality of being of this man and woman. Entirely different, yet fully matched in power. It was an exhilarating scene, and soon everyone was involved. We four sat, gawking as the commotion increased to a feverish pitch, then gradually subsided into mutterings and gesturings. Five minutes later, all was as before. The various participants in the fracas wandered off to their affairs, quite a few coming to circle around us, poking curiously into our gear, trying to communicate with us. The women hovered in the background.

We felt uncomfortable eating in front of our audience, knowing how nearly they starved here. So, we waited until it began to get dark, to pull out our stores of cheese and crackers and peanuts. Frank managed to arrange with some children to bring us a little firewood for a fire. Twig by tiny twig, a small stack materialized, brought by several little boys. Frank gave them a few coins, and it was apparent that they were the first they had held in their hands. I wondered what on earth they would do with money here.

Frank finally had enough hot water to make tea, and by the time that was done, most of the villagers had left. In the darkness we began to settle for sleep, which was not easy, given that the courtyard of this house was sloping and crisscrossed with irrigation ditches leading to a nearby cornfield.

As we were finally calming down, we heard a sudden scurrying. A boy appeared with what seemed to be a tray with a big bowl and three smaller bowls on it. He brought it over to where we were arranging our beds, and putting the tray on the ground, backed away shyly.

The big bowl, judging from the aroma, contained a boiled chicken. We simply sat there stunned. Then Klaus pulled out his flashlight to see what the boy had brought. It was indeed a tiny, whole chicken, mainly bones with just the barest amount of meat, in a broth. We had been given one of the few desperately thin and wretched chickens we had seen scratching in the dirt.

The four of us had our hands in that chicken so fast that it was gone, gulped, wolfed down in less than a minute. We shared out the broth and gulped that down, too, then sat back in silence.

When we could talk again, we spoke of our feverish behavior over the whole extraordinary situation.

Later, in our sleeping bags, we became hilarious. We made silly remarks and laughed hysterically. Then, Frank, serious, private New Zealander, began to make funny side comments to us about an old crone who apparently had crept up to his sleeping bag and was poking him. I was never quite sure if there really was such an old lady, or if it was all part of the hysteria.

But when, after a bit, I felt it was dark enough for me to tiptoe over to the nearby hedge to relieve myself, and stepped right into the mud and water of one of the irrigation ditches, it was just too much. The three men broke up in laughter as I swore and complained, and what remnants of decorum I had clung to, evaporated. We were of the land now, and accepting its dominance over us. The more we could accommodate to it, the more energy we would have to work our way home again.

Descending the Yarkun Valley, looking back
to where we have been

XXI

We could not leave the next day until we had taken everyone's picture. We finally understood that we were camped in the courtyard of relatives of the two brothers who were guiding us. So, nothing would do but that they should all stand in a row for the camera except the younger women, who hung back, discreetly distant.

Frank took several photographs, cajolling and talking, grouping them this way and that. By now, much of their shyness had faded, and the faces looking into the camera were excited and eager, big grins revealing more gums than teeth. Even a couple of old grannies sidled up to be included. Anonymous behind their veils, they were still enormously pleased thus to be recognized, judging from their tittering.

At last all the formalities were completed. We gave our hosts the jerry-can of kerosene, having no use for it, and our rice, which we could not cook, and a bag of dehydrated milk. These gifts were received with as much delight as we had felt over the chicken they had cooked for us, so by the time we marched off down the path, we were feeling pretty cheerful. Today we would walk to Mastuj, where there was a police station, and according to the officer we had met the day before, a jeep road and jeep, as Jahangir had reported. From Mastuj, it was about one hundred miles to Chitral, where we could get a plane out of the Himalayas. If the jeep could travel at about ten miles per hour, we might even be able to make Chitral by the evening of the next day. No wonder we felt hopeful.

"Ins'allah!" said Tom, in response to Frank's optimistic speculation.

117

Today was going to be hotter even than yesterday, because the valley was ever widening, the sky was clear, and the mountains being more modest here, the sun could climb over them earlier. After an hour or two of direct sun, we were no longer talking, and our enthusiastic march dwindled to a trudge. The path followed a definite pattern now of climbing up a ridge and descending the other side, and our knees and thighs were beginning to suffer from the downhills.

At one point we had a choice of paths. Either we could climb another ridge, switchbacking our way up several hundred feet, or we could proceed straight ahead into the river. Here, as in many places, there was room at the base of the cliff for a track along the edge of the river when it was running at normal depth. With the recent heavy rains, however, the river had risen about a foot over the path. We stood, indecisive, at the point where it went underwater. The thought of going up, and especially down, the ridge that rose above us made the prospect of wet feet look not so bad. So we elected the underwater track. The river was running fast, and there was a considerable drop-off into deep water at the edge of the path. The inevitable rolling rocks that constituted the surface contributed to treacherous footing.

I sighed to myself as I watched and felt the water come over the tops of my boots, and heard Klaus complain that he was afraid he would lose his loafers entirely. Tom splashed along in his tennis shoes, followed by Frank, who never complained about anything.

The donkeys waggled their ears and proceeded carefully, with the young brothers slopping along behind them in their too-big plastic oxfords.

After a quarter mile or so, the track climbed high enough to come out of the river, and we continued in our wet, miserably chafing shoes. Still, we had escaped one climb at least.

For a while the track stayed near the river and we trudged along without conversation. then, another river came down from the ridge to intersect the Yarkun, forming a sort of delta of grey sludge silt. The donkeys were ahead of us here, and advanced into the sludge. And sank.

It was amazing how quickly they sank into what turned out to

be quicksand. What stopped them from sinking out of sight immediately were the duffle-bags hanging on their sides, which acted like
floats.

So there they were, sunk to their bellies, looking at us with
their liquid eyes and waving their ears. We could only stand helplessly and stare. The two boys, without hesitation, threw their shoes
on the bank, peeled off their pin-stripe jackets, and jumped to the
rescue. Shouting, and shoving wildly, they threw themselves at the
donkeys with so much momentum that all four of them suddenly
were in the river beyond. Here the water was running fast, and the
footing became sound again. As the donkeys and boys climbed up on
the bank out of the river, dripping mud and water, we realized more
fully what could have happened.

Impressed by the resourcefulness of these two young men, we
stood by respectfully while they reorganized the donkeys, put on
their shoes and jackets, and started off again.

Soon after this we began an ascent through apple trees, ter-
raced corn, and a few huts. Halfway up, the boys stopped us and
gestured to a path that angled off through the trees. "Chai," they said.
We demurred, wanting not to lose our momentum, but they insisted
so firmly that it seemed we must stop. Frank, Tom, and I went along,
but Klaus was adamant in his refusal, and remained on the main path
to dry out his shoes a little.

We were led under the trees to a really pleasant terrace in front
of a hut, with trees hanging over us, leafy and cool, and full of
apples. We helped ourselves while the old man who greeted us went
off to arrange for tea. In time he came back with the donkey drivers
and an old woman carrying a small tray with the tea.

The cups were an offshade and cracked, the tea was quite hot
and heavily sugared, and we drank it gratefully. After we finished the
tea, the old woman took the cups and washed them in the irrigation
ditch that ran through the terrace. In silence we watched her, and
noticed at the same time the wild life and garbage flowing along in the
ditch. We looked at each other, somewhat glumly, but there was
nothing to be done. So we sat back and ate apples.

After a while the brothers got up to leave, and with much smil-

119

ing and nodding all around, we trooped back to the main path. We never did find out what that stop was all about. Presumably another relative, and another example of firm Himalayan hospitality.

We found Klaus, in bare feet, standing on the path and taking a picture of a goat high in a tree, all four feet wedged in a crotch of branches. The goat was with calm aplomb helping himself to apples. He looked down at us, yellow eyes glinting, and shook his ridiculous goatee as if to say, "What's the matter? Didn't you ever see a goat climb a tree before?"

Klaus put on his still-wet shoes and we continued up, then down the ridge. After a long march, with the sun so full on us that I could think of nothing else, we came to a small village that, for a brief moment, I thought was our destination. Of course, it was not, but the donkey drivers did motion us to stop and rest on a field of what seemed to be grass, the first we had seen in our whole trip. There were a few apple trees here and there, apparently mostly for shade. The area seemed to be a park. The whole feeling was of approaching civilization, and we were encouraged.

The boys picked more apples for us; we had one last can of cheese to go with our crackers and peanuts, and we lay on the grass gratefully.

Soon we were marching again, and now came an awful stretch of sun-blasted rocky plains. They were rolling and uneven as the track rose and descended. My legs began to give out. I was having to stop often now, collapsing even in the full sun to rest. My knees discovered a new trick here. When I would get up, after a five-minute stop, my legs would jackknife, remain in a 45° angle, and would not straighten out. I would have to hobble like that, with my legs half bent for several minutes until gradually the frozen muscles would limber up and release their cramp. It was a painful process, yet the desire to sit down every twenty minutes or so was so great that it overrode the apprehension of bent knees.

This section was endless, it seemed. Again beaten by sun and exhaustion, and increasingly dehydrated, I felt my courage draining away. It was getting harder and harder to find water that was not full of floating things, so we were not drinking enough. Finally, of course, we began to accept the inevitable, and to fill our bottles from the irrigation ditches, floating things and all. Presumably that's what the iodine crystals were for; we hoped we were not asking too much of them.

It was not until about midafternoon that we saw the village of Mastuj. The most prominent feature was a telephone line that ran from one large building in the center of town on down the valley. Now we knew we were getting somewhere.

A second large river came into a 'Y' with the Yarkun, forming a plateau on which Mastuj was sitting. It was really a town, the largest settlement we had seen since we left Gilgit, a couple of weeks before. We increased our pace, heading toward that magic telephone line.

Distance was deceptive in that so clear Himalayan air, and we marched for another hour before coming into town. We began to pass people who were politely curious, but did not stop to stare as the people of the remote valleys had. Crossing a broad field in front of an aluminum-roofed empty building, perhaps a schoolhouse, we saw a young blonde woman coming toward us. She was dressed in western hiking gear, and carried a pack. As she came up to us, we stopped and, glad to see a western face again, greeted her with some enthusiasm. She looked at us coolly, and kept going. Astonished, we turned to watch her receding back. Frank called out, "Where's the police station?"

"Not far," came her voice, floating back. Briskly she marched away along the path we had just come down.

"Well!" said Tom. "What's her problem?"

Klaus said, "She's probably a dope dealer and doesn't want to get into any questions from us."

"Do you think she's American?" I said.

"Her English is pretty good; could be," said Tom.

"Well still, she could have said 'Hello' or something," I said.

Frank said, "Well, at least it isn't far."

I had heard that before, and was believing nothing until I saw it myself, these days. And, sure enough, we trundled along the broad paths of Mastuj for the best part of another hour before we found the

121

police station. People pointed it out to us as we proceeded, in response to our "Police station?" and exhausted appearances. To our joy we saw dust being stirred up here and there by speeding jeeps, though they were too far away to attempt to contact a driver.

Finally, as late afternoon shadowed the little town, we found ourselves in the police station, pulling out our dirty letter from Jahangir, and trying to understand the rudimentary English of the officer in charge.

"Can we get a jeep?" Frank asked. The by-now large crowd of policemen looked blank.

"We want a jeep to Chitral," said Frank patiently.

"No jeep." Firmly. The police official who seemed to be in charge shook his head, back and forth, "No jeep."

I sat down on a rickety chair and burst into tears. The men of my group looked at me, and Klaus said, "That won't help."

What did I care? I had run out of energy for unpleasant surprises. I felt like crying, so I did.

The Pakistani policemen looked at me impassively.

"No jeep."

It seems that the monsoon rains had destroyed the jeep road. Piece by piece, the story came clear. First we all had to have tea. Then the police captain had to show off his telephone by calling Chitral to discuss the road. They were cut off twice before completing their conversation (largely a matter of laughter and hilarity, presumably about the weird foreigners).

"No jeep."

I sagged into a stupor. It would take eight or ten more days to walk to Chitral.

XXII

One of Jock's doomsday comments came floating back to me.

"Remember," he said, "this is not Nepal. There are no rescue units on every corner here. If you fall down and break a leg, or get pulmonary edema, we'll try to get you out somehow, but it could take days. Weeks, even."

With Jock's voice in my ears, I asked the police captain anyway, "Could we get a helicopter?"

He looked at me without expression, and lifted his shoulders slightly.

"No helicopter."

Of course. It was enough of a problem in lower altitudes bringing in one or two planes in the earliest morning when the air is at its densest. There were no helicopters even in Rawalpindi as I remembered back.

Yet I truly did not believe I could go another week or more as we had travelled these last days. The heat was ever more oppressive, under even more hours per day of full sun as the valley widened out. The altitude, by now eight or nine thousand feet, still kept my edema troublesome. I had utterly run out of gas. An overnight rest would allow me a few hours walking the next morning, but we would have to march at least seven or eight hours a day to get out in a week.

I slumped, uncaring that by now the room was jammed with all sorts of interested people, some in uniform, some not. I did not even try to hold myself intact under their staring; instead I just let them help themselves to me. I was beyond caring. I knew I was a strange sight, with torn and filthy clothes that I had not taken off

123

even at night for a week. Uncombed hair, stiff with dirt, swollen face probably smeared with tears and dust. Perhaps even my teeth were green; I could not remember the last time I had brushed them. It did not matter. Nothing mattered except that I should not have to walk any more.

Suddenly I heard myself say, "What about horses?" The others looked at me, as did the police officer. It was clear that this idea was plausible.

And, after much haranguing, hesitation, dubious headshaking, it was arranged.

For a high fee, by local standards, though for me no price was too high, it was settled that we would have four horses at five the next morning, and two donkeys with their drivers. Our two brothers and their donkeys would go no farther from home than here in Mastuj, and were waiting outside with our gear for directions where to unload.

A contract in English and Urdu was written and signed by the police captain; everyone smiled and nodded, and we were led out of the office. A young policeman took us to a place in the barracks where we could sleep. I felt strange, a woman in the police living quarters, and was roundly gawked at as I followed the others demurely. The buildings were like all dwellings in these mountains, only larger. A connected series of mud-walled and roofed rooms opened only in front onto a verandah. We were taken into one of the small windowless rooms. It was dark and smelled extremely badly. It had an inside door tied shut with a stout rope, knotted so securely that we understood we were to stay out. Human curiosity was stirred by the forbidden room, and we tried to peer through the crack around the door frame, as soon as the policeman was out of the room. Tom fell back, gasping.

"It's a latrine," he said, making a face. I decided not to try to look after all.

It did not make much difference that the latrine door was closed. The room stank. It is a lucky thing sometimes that human senses are so adaptable. Soon we hardly noticed the smell.

124

We went out and negotiated with our young donkey drivers. Besides the agreed upon price, Klaus gave the younger boy his boots and an elegant red silk scarf he had brought from Switzerland twenty-five years before. The boy smiled and smiled. What he would do with size thirteen boots was not clear, but it *was* clear that he saw them as a great prize.

We all handed out gifts of one sort or another to the two boys, feeling sorry to see them go. They had brought us a long way and we were grateful.

The men began to discuss the prospect of riding horses, and all three were anxious about it. None had ridden much, and they were agreed that horses were dangerous and stupid.

I, on the other hand, was so relieved at the thought of not having to walk any more that I could have cried all over again. Furthermore, I grew up on horses and could ride all day without ill effect. I had grown up with a great pleasure in Arabian horses, their pretty heads, slim legs and straight short backs. While most of my experience had been on quarter horses, I had long yearned after the trim elegance of the Arab.

As a child I had read a book called *Drinkers of the Wind*, all about a man's search through the Middle East for the prototype of the Arabian horse as it is known in the West. After much travelling, the author came to understand that the tiny tough horses he saw everywhere, dragging or carrying great loads, were indeed the Arab prototype. His inflated image of the glorious ancestor he had expected to find was dispelled. In its place came a grudging appreciation for the modest yet valiant little horse he did discover.

I had seen only an occasional horse as we came down the Yarkun Valley, perhaps three or four in all. They were very thin, as tall as my shoulder, and all were stallions. They had the lovely dish face classic to the Arabian horse, the trim strong legs and short coupling that was familiar to me. But they were scrawny, with great protruding hip bones, ratty tails, thin necks, which made me sad about the rough existence they had here.

Then I looked again at the people who worked their lives out in this wild terrain, saw their thin bodies and bony extremities, their

125

goiters and blind eyes, and felt better. The people did not live at their animals' expense; it was a shared endurance.

My spirits had risen so much that when Tom pulled out his only pair of long pants for riding and saw how totally ripped and ragged they were, I volunteered to try to patch them up for him.

I was myself surprised. I had reached a point long since of having no energy to do anything for anyone, not even for myself. So I could hardly believe the renewed interest I felt. My own pants were torn in the seat, too, worn threadbare in the marching. I had begun with two pairs of nearly new pants, and the first pair had torn hopelessly already a week before.

I found a needle and thread, and dressed in a big baggy pair of Klaus's pants, took Tom's and my torn clothes out on the verandah where there was light enough to sew. By pooling all our ripped clothes, I was able to organize enough patching material to make both Tom and me decent again, if somewhat gypsy-like.

A policeman who had been lying on his charpoi on the verandah outside our room offered to let me sit on it. Somewhat gingerly, I climbed onto this strange piece of furniture that I had seen all over the mountains, as well as in Delhi, Lahore, and everywhere else in this part of the world.

It was a delight; a wooden frame, strung with hemp like a hammock and covered with rugs and blankets. I perched on it cross-legged with my sewing and felt entirely comfortable. Several policemen watched me work, examining my small scissors carefully, then returning them to me. For whatever reason, I ascribed magic properties to the charpoi that brought me comfort and rest.

By the time I had finished, it was nearly dark. We prepared our bedrolls on the dirt floor of the cell-like room, ate our peanuts and crackers, and finally it was dark enough to look for "bathroom" facilities. With so little to eat and drink, and so much physical exertion and heat, we could all wait for long intervals for such facilities. A good thing, too, since nowadays we were always under scrutiny.

Klaus and I went out together with a flashlight. We tiptoed around the sleeping men on the verandah, slipped out the front gate of the compound and around to the back where we had seen a corn-field. We each made our way into the corn in the by now familiar way, completed our business and came out. I saw a shape move near-by and touched Klaus's arm. He looked and laughed softly.

"It seems to be everyone's bathroom."

And so it was. We cautioned Tom and Frank to be careful where they stepped, and they went out with the flashlight.

At least the floor was flat and smooth here, and we had only its hardness to adapt to. Our great fatigue finally overrode discomfort and we slept.

And came wildly awake soon after to the noise of someone coming into our room. Shocked and groggy we peered into the dim light of a small kerosene lamp. One of the policemen had come with a tray of tea.

The anomaly of it all undid us. We laughed and greeted the young man, and in great exuberance gulped down the sugary warm tea, and thanked the shy policeman warmly.

He withdrew and we went quickly back to sleep.

The author on the small Arab horse, prototye of our
Western Arabian horse, with its owner

XXIII

Actually, none of us slept for long after that. After dozing for an hour or so, I began to shift and turn over, trying to get comfortable. I heard the others doing the same.

"What time is it?"

"One-thirty."

We whispered to each other for comfort. Sleeping on the dust floor of a jail cell was not easy, and our whispers reassured us that we were there voluntarily. Sometimes we could hear the creak and groan of someone turning over on his charpoi on the verandah outside our window. But the joking and sniggering we shared reassured us.

At last the deep darkness of the Himalayan night began to yield to early dawn. About four o'clock we began to roll up our beds, eat our peanuts and crackers, drink our foul-tasting water. The horses were to come at five and we wanted to be ready.

We made our trips to the cornfield, collected our gear and tip-toed out past the sleeping policemen. Outside the main gate of the police station, we piled up our belongings and stood uncertainly. We were on the edge of a bare field, perhaps a parade ground, with corn-fields and modest huts around its perimeter.

We waited. Nothing and nobody moved. Dawn came on fully, and still we waited.

Around six, a police officer came out. Frank asked him about the horses; he shrugged, then called to a man who had been peering out at us from the safety of the gate.

The man, in response to an order from the officer, took off

across the field at a run and disappeared around a cornfield. A few minutes later he reappeared and said something to the officer.

"Eating breakfast," said the officer. So we waited some more.

Eventually a single rider appeared on a small grey horse. When he reached us and climbed down, it became clear that this was it. We all looked at each other. After a moment, the three men agreed to let me use the horse, while they would continue walking.

Feeling only slightly guilty, I climbed up on the horse, somewhat concerned that he would have trouble with my weight. He was so narrow I was afraid he would collapse under me.

On the contrary, he danced around and seemed quite interested in his new rider, sniffing my boot and flicking his ears. It was like coming home to be up on this thin little stallion, although the contrast in his size to the stocky quarter horses I had grown up on was a bit worrisome. It soon became clear to me, though, that this scrawny grey Arab was as enduring as any well-fed western horse.

His owner, equally tiny, and emaciated and old-looking, walked alongside the horse and me, with a hand on his horse's neck. We started off, and soon left the others behind, including by now our two new donkeys and their drivers.

The track we were following led in the direction opposite to our destination. It kept close to the second river which formed the "Y" with the Yarkun at Mastuj. We had to find a bridge across it in order to continue along the Yarkun down to Chitral. There once was a bridge big enough for jeeps right at Mastuj, but monsoon floods had washed it out three years earlier, and there was no sign of reconstruction. About three miles away we came to a long, high footbridge that spanned the wide vigorous river. My guide motioned me down off the horse, and I followed nervously along after them as they picked their way slowly over it. The horse sniffed and snorted some, but stepped steadily across, so I decided it must be safe. The swaying motion was disturbing, however, to say the least.

I remounted on the other side and looked back across the river to see if the others were coming. Two were trudging along behind the donkeys and their owners. Farther back was a horse with a big man up on him. Judging from the size, the rider had to be Klaus, and my sympathies were stirred. Klaus had grown up in civilized Europe, and his sport was skiing. Horses and all the vagaries of nature made him nervous. He had no idea what to expect, and turning himself over to an animal as large as a horse was not a happy experience for him.

Although, in this case, I had to grin. He looked, from a distance, as big as the horse. Hunched in the saddle, with his long legs jackknifed in the short stirrups, he fairly enveloped the horse. Except for the terrors of the track we were to follow, he might find he could hold his own with this animal.

As we went behind a ridge, I lost sight of the others and began to pay attention to my own situation. The path was extremely narrow, with some loose rocks on it, though it was well-travelled. From early training I knew the importance of letting the horse decide how to proceed, particularly if he is native to the area. So I let the reins go slack and tried not to think about the dangers of stumbling and falling down what was an ever increasing distance to the river below.

In general this attitude worked well. The only difficulty was when we would meet another traveller. If it was someone on foot, my horse would stiffen a bit and dance. His owner would grab the bridle and growl something, and we would get safely by, though the dancing took us out on the lip of the path.

But another horse approaching was very alarming. I began to realize that all horses being ridden were stallions; though there had to be mares in these mountains, too, none were in evidence. Perhaps, like the women, mares were kept in seclusion. At a meeting of my stallion with another, the excitement would boil over, as in any part of the world, and the two would enter at once into a supremacy struggle.

Such squealing and half-rearing, and laid-back ears would go on, the two owners tugging and shouting. All I could do was sit tight, and trust the men to control the horses. It was terrifying to be pitched around in their frenzy on a track perhaps two feet wide with only an occasional wider space for two horses to pass.

After the first couple of incidents I did begin to believe that the men knew how to contain their animals well enough, and that if I would just ride it out, everything would be all right.

131

Luckily it was not until some time later that we listened to a friend talk about his trek with a group in the Andes, and a horse that fell on both the woman riding it and the guide. The woman's ankle was dislocated and a leg bone was broken and sticking through the skin. Our friend had walked out at double speed and with much confusion and persuasion finally was able to arrange for a helicopter two days later. That he could locate a helicopter at all was extraordinary, and then the pick-up to be made on the side of a mountain at an altitude of fifteen thousand feet was a further nightmare.

It was just as well for my nervous frame of mind that I trusted my horse and guide as much as I did, since there was nothing to be done anyway. Unless I wanted to walk again. So I shut up and rode.

After a while we stopped at a wide place near a cornfield and hut complex. Klaus came up and so finally did Tom and Frank. While we stood there we saw another man on a horse approaching. Finally we understood the plan. The arrangement for horses was that we would collect them one by one as we went along. Apparently there were very few horses this high up the valley, and some of the haggling the evening before was to figure out how to get us to the horses.

Sure enough, about an hour later, by now late morning, a fourth horse was ridden up to us, and Frank, too, climbed on.

It was a funny sight, which, now that I was off my feet and up on a horse, I could fully appreciate. The three men, all tall, were scrunched into tiny saddles designed for men half their size, knees up under their chins, and wretchedness in their faces. My own situation was not perfect; my legs also were too long, but by sitting up on the back of the saddle, the cantle, I could more or less straighten out my knees and thereby brace myself against the jolting and uneven motion of my horse as he maneuvered the difficult path.

By now we had left the cultivated area that extended out around Mastuj and began to climb the inevitable ridges that intercepted the river periodically. We could see that this was indeed a jeep road, and that it was indeed washed out. Each ridge that extended out and down from the mountains that ran along the river was succeeded by a ravine that had been swept out by the rains. The narrowest of footpaths had been hacked out in each of these; men were working to that purpose as we came through. On a couple of occasions we had to wait while they cut a path for us. As could be expected it was a minimum passage, and not packed down at all. The horses slipped and stumbled along, and sometimes we were directed to get off so the guides could lead them across some particularly perilous place.

Heights were, as usual, frightening, and as usual, the river was roaring angrily along below. Heat poured down on us; our water supplies were low. When my dour little guide pulled out small wormy apples from his voluminous pajama suit, I ate them with scarcely a qualm. They did help.

As we climbed, descended, stumbled and picked our way through the again desolate terrain, I had a chance to study this silent man. He appeared to be about sixty, dark, not more than five feet tall, and expressionless. His gnarled hand lay flat on his horse's neck and was cracked and leathery. His stamina was awesome. Hour after hour, mile after mile, he marched along, keeping pace with the horse—and periodically fed me apples from a seemingly endless supply.

By midafternoon he seemed to soften slightly. I think he noticed my appreciation of his horse, and the fact that I was at home on horseback. As he handed me apples he would almost smile, and actually look at me. Then later, as we came to a small village, he was joined by another man about his age. We all stopped while these two men greeted each other in what seemed to be the local tradition. They stopped, facing each other, and each put his right hand flat on the heart of the other. After a moment they embraced briefly, then turned and walked along the wide village track, holding hands. I rode along behind them, touched. I had seen this form of greeting higher up the valley, and was charmed by the gentleness of the exchange in this tough world.

One of the donkey drivers spoke some English, and noting my interest, said, "They are brothers."

The two venerable men walked along, hand in hand, for a mile or two, chatting and laughing together. When we were well out of the village, the local man stopped and waved, then turned back as we went on.

As the shadows began to slant more and more across our path, the donkey driver came up to where Klaus and I were riding side by side on a broad part of the track. Grinning widely, he said, "You like chicken?"

We snapped to attention.

"Yes!"

"You can buy chicken for dinner at Awi, where we will stop."

We were excited. Giving the young man our full attention we explored the possibilities. Yes, we could get a chicken cooked for us, and potatoes, and tomatoes. Yes, we could have two chickens and yes, lots of potatoes.

Frank and Tom, riding behind us, made dubious noises.

"I don't know about that. I'm a little afraid of it," said Frank.

Klaus and I could not have been less concerned about the safety of local food. By now, we had eaten so many filthy apples obviously picked up off the ground, drunk so much foul water, been in contact one way or another with so many surfaces presumably swarming with friendly and unfriendly organisms, we were hardly going to worry about a cooked chicken.

Anyway, discussing our evening menu kept us totally distracted for the balance of the trip. By the time we were settled at the Rest House at Awi we were obsessed. Even the fact that we each were given a charpoi to sleep on, and that there was a more or less clear stream running through the place to wash in, did not matter. What did matter was choosing among the squawking, flapping, mangy little chickens offered up by the feet by an assortment of citizens, men, women, and children. We finally selected three of the miserably bony birds, and gave them to the young man who would presumably cook them, somehow, somewhere.

An hour later, there it was—perhaps the best meal I will ever have. Mainly bones, but what meat there was on those chickens was delicious. A seasoned broth, a painfully small dish of potatoes, sliced and boiled, another dish of tomato slices. We were eating by kerosene light, so whatever distressing dirt or foreign matter we may have swallowed with our food was invisible. Though even if we had seen it, nothing could have stopped me from wolfing that food. Frank and

Tom also seemed to overcome their hesitancy, and to Klaus's and my disappointment, dug right in.

Though we could have eaten the same meal several times over, we did end up with a lovely comforted feeling of having been well-fed. As we unrolled our sleeping bags on the charpois we chatted amiably. It was the first experience of contentment since we began this whole adventure.

Then I stretched out on the rug-covered hemp webbing of the charpoi and could not believe the comfort. So used, by now, to trying to accommodate hips and shoulders to unyielding, sloped ground with rocks embedded in it, I could scarcely comprehend the way the charpoi accommodated to me.

Even without nine hours of horse-riding behind me, I would have sunk immediately into sleep. As it was, I went out like a light.

From Thui An Pass

XXIV

Tom's whisper woke me up. The utter darkness confused me, and it took a moment to recognize just what had wakened me.

I remembered then. The night before our guides had informed us that they wanted to be on the way by four in the morning. It would take seven or eight hours riding to reach the Army Ranger Station where jeeps could be arranged for. The guides wanted to be able to return to Awi by early evening of the same day. We were willing, since it meant that we would have several hours travel in the cool.

My watch said three-thirty. The flashlight's yellow beam was all the light there was. The stars were brilliant in the clear night sky, but their illumination was negligible for our purpose. Complaining and giggling, we gathered up our belongings mostly by touch. While we did so, I vaguely remembered music and laughter during the night as several groups of people came to the Rest House for some sort of gathering. They had not really disturbed me, though, as my great fatigue had overridden everything, especially given the boon of a good bed. Now by flashlight, I could see still forms rolled up in blankets all around us in the courtyard.

We did make an effort to subdue our own noise, but our blind stumbling around elicited a certain amount of commentary from us.

"Where's my damn boot?"

"Oh, ick, there's squashed apple all over my sleeping bag. I must have slept on it."

"Ouch! I stubbed my toe!"

"Lovely taste in my mouth."

But last night's party-goers slept peacefully throughout our

137

departure preparations. We climbed up on the horses, directed by our guides to the right ones since they were indistinguishable to us in the dark. The donkey drivers somehow got our gear loaded on the donkeys, and we were indeed on our way by four o'clock.

The guides must have known the track intimately. They led our horses right out, and we sat in our saddles absolutely helpless. I could not even see the old man leading my horse. Yet he seemed to know or see exactly where we were. My horse did not stumble or hesitate; he walked right along with his master.

Rocks clattered underfoot, and sometimes we splashed through streams. I strained to see in the blackness, and saw nothing. There is essentially no electric light in these Himalayas and the darkness was nearly total as a result. In the West we are usually within some range of artificial light that provides at least a dim illusion of illumination. Here, in this biblical world, nothing. The night was absolute.

We four spoke little to each other; I felt there was only my horse and me in the whole world. It was not unpleasant; it was rather like being suspended in time and space.

Gradually, of course, there was a lightening and I could distinguish my guide with his hand on my horse's neck. Then the scenery emerged from the grey of earliest dawn. Distant mountains ahead of us were still totally black, and those on either side of the valley we were descending also showed up as black profiles without features.

Then, at a turn in the road, I looked ahead, and sucked in my breath. Rising up and up from the top of the group of tall black mountains far ahead, shone a brilliant pyramid of sunlit snow. A monster peak, thousands of feet higher than its tall neighbors, caught the rising sun and was struck by a red-tinged illumination that shocked me into blankness. I took in the sight like a blow to my flesh and bones. For minutes my horse carried me along as I looked, mesmerized, at that appalling snow peak.

Finally I came to and realized that it was Tirich Mir, more than twenty-five thousand feet high, and the sentinel of Chitral. It was at least a hundred miles away, yet it filled the sky. The combination of

138

the sheer majesty of the mountain and the extraordinary coincidence of sunrise and our position had created this stunning moment. I see it now as I did then. It is forever imprinted in my imagination, emblematic of a time out of mind.

I twisted around in my saddle and saw Klaus's reaction to the scene, and he nodded. I turned back, and we all rode without speaking for a time, watching Tirich Mir.

It still hung in the air above us when we were brought to a halt at a small roadside building. We were instructed to dismount, which we did somewhat stiffly. It was eight o'clock and I became aware of hunger.

"Tea, here," said one of the guides, and directed us to a table and chairs outside the building. We stretched and sat, wondering what next.

It turned out to be another police station, and Frank went off with the captain to tell our story. We waited, fishing out our so-stale crackers and eternal peanuts. In time, a small boy came out with a tea tray. The cracked china, the flies walking on the sweet tea drops everywhere, the lukewarm milky tea itself, all was as usual.

Shortly, Frank reappeared. All was well, and we were told to get back up on our horses. We were taken through village after village, past cornfields, huts, children, men, long trains of loaded donkeys, many with bells and gay decorations on their heads and saddles. Life was stirring everywhere, in the fields, the fruit trees, courtyards and the increasing number of shops. Tom even found a small shop selling cigarettes.

After a few hours, we were led off the main track and brought into a pleasant tree-shaded yard. We got down and sat around on the charpois as seemed to be expected of us. An older man greeted us with "salaam" and bows, and with a sweep of his arm, ordered a younger man off to get something.

In time he reappeared with a tray of chapattis, tea, and mulberries. We were intrigued and grateful for the change of diet, and ate everything offered. There were some efforts at conversaton, but the difficulty was not only the lack of vocabulary in common, but also the absence of experience in common. What is there to communicate about, when, in the few minutes of a shared meal, there is the need to span hundreds of years of divergent history? We settled for smiles and nods, and expressions of appreciation, and when we left we knew that they, like us, knew no more than before of the experience of the others. On the other hand, there was an undeniable sharing of the simple warmth of one human for another and the visit did provide that comfort.

Just as we were beginning to relax now that the worst was over, we started to climb again. Looking ahead, we could see a great sequence of ridges ranged across our way. Again we would have to ascend and descend ridge after ridge. The sun was above now; there were no more orchards or green to relieve the scene. We were still in the Himalayas and faced with the continued effort to withstand the sun, the heat, and the exertion. But we had Tirich Mir beckoning to us now, and where Tirich Mir was, there was Chitral and an airstrip. We were coming out of the mountains at long last.

XXV

As we traversed a great cliff, our horses plodding along the narrow track in the midday sun, we saw the Ranger Station. It emerged as a sprawling encampment far below us alongside the Yarkun River.

An hour later we were there and stopped at its gates. We rolled stiffly off our horses and stood around uncertainly. Then Frank, our unofficial leader and nanny, went to the guard to make our request for a jeep. He was not permitted entry beyond a few feet, but an officer did come to talk with him. A few minutes later, Frank returned to us, saying that he had been assured by the officer that a jeep would be along soon to take us to Chitral.

We did not understand whether the rangers would be providing the jeep, or whether there was a regular commercial jeep-run into Chitral, about fifty miles away. The horses we had ridden and their owners were crowded around us, wanting their money, so we decided to settle that account while we waited for the jeep.

The settling-up was difficult. Over the two days' journey their price had doubled, in spite of the written and signed contract drawn up in the Mastuj police station. There was much haranguing and shouting; one horse owner and the donkey driver in particular were angry with the original agreement. It was hard to tell where the obligatory haggling left off and genuine distress began. By now we had collected a considerable audience: rangers in their English style khaki uniforms with berets, local people in their cotton pajama suits. Someone came with a huge plate full of grapes as tiny as currants. It was necesary to pick them off many at a time with one's teeth, since

141

they were too small to pick off one at a time in the fingers. It was a messy, sticky treat, but it was a treat.

I do not know who gave them to us. Perhaps the bargaining process demanded refreshment, because a little while later a tray of tea was brought. By now we were sitting at a distance from the Ranger Station on benches and charpois, in front of a small shop. I had an uneasy feeling we would be there for quite a while.

And so we were. We finally settled with the horse and donkey owners; they jumped up on their animals and took off at great speed to return, not to Awi after all, but all the way back to Mastuj that night. We were awed by the extraordinary strength and endurance of the Himalayans, man and beast. When they were gone, we felt again our tenuous position with no mediators between us and the strange surroundings.

The audience gathered about us moved in a little closer, as if sensing our vulnerability. They settled down, apparently to wait and see what the foreigners would do next.

After some discussion we asked the one or two who spoke a little English how to get a jeep. Sure enough, there would have been no jeep if we had relied on the ranger's statement. A man volunteered to run to the next town to try to round up a jeep and its driver. The sun was pounding down; the man was not young, and the fee we offered was modest. He seemed willing, however, so we watched guiltily as he disappeared, trotting, in search of transportation for us.

An hour later he reappeared, riding triumphantly in the back of a small jeep. We four piled our gear into the jeep, struck a bargain with the driver in erratic pigeon and body English, then climbed on top of the lugguage. To our consternation, three men jumped onto the jeep too, two in with us, the third standing on the rear bumper clinging to an upright for safety. They smiled meltingly at us, gesturing piteously for our indulgence.

There was nothing to do, given our alien situation, but to accept the newcomers as our guests and get on. So there were eight of us, plus gear, crammed into the jeep. Perhaps it was just as well that the fit was so tight, because the trip was wild. Had we been loosely packed, we might well have lost someone on a turn.

Trekking the Hindu Kush

For a few miles, the road was all right. That is, it ran along the river with plenty of room. Then we began to climb cliffs as the valley narrowed. The river became a cataract in its channel; the road became again a matter of improvisation. The twig, rock, twig layering in a cantilevered fashion terrified us all again, particularly since this driver was not under the supervision of our tour leader. He went much faster than the earlier drivers, and we were stiff with fear. In and out, up and down, the jeep careened along the cliff faces.

At one point, there was a series of turns that were too tight even for a jeep. The driver had to back and fill several times in order to get around. There were, of course, no guard rails of any sort, and on one of these perilous turns I looked down to the bottom of the ravine to see several smashed jeeps. Tom laughed hollowly.

"They seem to have plenty of jeeps to spare!" I closed my eyes.

Then opened them quickly. I wanted to keep watch, as if it would help to keep the driver on the road. Suddenly, he stopped the jeep. We pitched forward, but were sufficiently wedged in so that no one was hurt. The driver climbed out into the few inches between the cliff and the jeep, and one of the other Himalayans climbed out, too. We were horrified when we realized the driver had something in his eye. His passenger peered into the driver's eye, lifting the lid to look for the offending particle. Soon they both got back in and we took off again at high speed. I wondered if the driver could see.

The drive to Chitral took four hours, and night was coming down as we approached the little town. As we drove along what appeared to be a main road toward town, the jeep died. I could not bear to think that we would get stuck now, in man-made machinery, after all we had come through.

The driver piled out of the jeep, carrying a gasoline can. He was unperturbed. It was as if he had planned his gas supply exactly, because we had passed a gas pump only a few hundred yards back. We leaned on each other and were actually glad for the respite in tension, and waited for the driver.

Ten minutes later he returned, pulled up the rubber floor mat in front of his seat, rolled it into a tube and poured the gasoline through this into the gas tank. Apparently the small amounts of dust and rocks that must have been washed into the tank too did no harm, because we were promptly on our way again.

A few minutes later we were standing in the middle of our luggage in the garden of the Tirich Mir Inn. English style, it was built in a square *u*-shape around lawns and flower beds. The proprietor came to greet us, and took us to our rooms. We had beds and bathrooms, and were overjoyed. I peeled my horrible clothing off and went to stand under the shower head. It was on a pipe extending from the wall to the middle of the room, with a drain underneath. I turned on the faucet and a trickle of cold water dropped on me. I gasped in shock. The sun was gone now and the air was chill. Yet clear water from a pipe was such a luxury that I stayed in it long enough to wash some of the filth from my hair and body. I felt exhilarated as I dried myself on the small towel that had been with me through the whole expedition. I was not much cleaner; my towel was pretty awful, but it was a start.

We met the others for dinner in the hotel's enormous dining room. It was quite empty, and our voices echoed. We were brought boiled chicken and potatoes and tomato slices by a silent waiter. It was nowhere near enough to fill our stomachs, but it was more than we were used to, and we were content. We fell silent, and felt our deep fatigue. Saying goodnight we parted for the first time in six days to go to separate sleeping quarters. It was a lovely thing to go behind a closed door. Klaus and I were asleep in minutes.

XXVI

There was a big bowl of cornflakes on the breakfast table, and I ate them all. The three men watched me, bemused, looking sleep-ridden. Scrambled eggs and tea arrived and I ate that, too.

In the dark, empty dining room, we four talked in whispers. Tom and Frank, incredibly, thought they would arrange a short tour up the Kaffiristan Valley, alongside the Afghanistan border. Klaus and I, on the other hand, had but one purpose. We wanted to go home.

Following the directions given by the concierge, we went into town to look for the Pakistan International Airlines Office. It was hard to imagine such a thing in this exotic dusty village. Chitral looked to me like one big bazaar. Nothing but open-front shops dispensing cooked food, raw materials, even, occasionally, western-looking products such as pots and pans and clothing.

Jeeps swirled through the streets raising dust, which then settled back on everything. Food, clothes, grains, all were layered in dust. Chitral was very much like Gilgit where we had begun our expedition several weeks earlier.

To expect to find an airlines office in such a place seemed unlikely, but we did eventually locate it. Of course, it was not like any airlines office I had ever seen before.

It was one small room with a stand-up desk near one wall, but this was hard to see because there must have been forty people in the room, pushing and arm-waving. The noise was awful; most people were shouting and cursing as well as shoving. Several nationalities were represented, Middle Eastern and Western. Young Europeans, strangely dressed and exaggeratedly made-up, were yelling in Swiss-German, Italian, English. Pakistanis in their Hunza hats, cotton paja-

145

mas, and plastic shoes leaned into the squalling mass of humanity, shouting their demands at two uniformed airlines officials. Clearly nothing could be accomplished here.

We looked at each other helplessly, shrugging in bewilderment. We stepped back, away from the din, and Klaus nearly bumped into a large, stocky Middle Easterner who had just emerged from another office. This man, perhaps in his sixties, was dressed like the others except for the addition of a fierce-looking double-barrelled shotgun. He held the weapon by the throat, muzzle pointing upward, and looked us over without expression. I was afraid of him, with his wild dark eyes and stern look. After a moment, he gestured with his gun in the direction of the office he had just left. Opening the door, he indicated that we should come in. In trepidation, we did, not knowing his purpose.

A leather couch and several chairs were ranged around a western style desk. He sat behind the desk and waved us to seats. For a moment we waited uncertainly, then sat. After another close inspection of us all, he put his gun in the corner behind him, and we relaxed a little.

"So what can I do for you?" It was not what we expected at all. I, for one, had had visions of abduction, or worse, having by now lost much of my self-confidence. I had become so vulnerable to my surroundings that it seemed plausible to worry in terms of abduction. Thereby doing the Shahzada a real injustice. For this man was the Prince of Chitral Province, with four hundred years of royalty behind him. The Province is an enormous region, technically part of Pakistan now, but in reality still an untamed Himalayan wilderness.

The Shahzada introduced himself to us, and had tea brought. He poured it for us, with slow ceremony, his dark face friendly now. People knocked at the door periodically and he dealt with them quickly. He seemed interested in us, asking us who we were, where we came from, what we were doing in the Himalayas. One of his activities was running the P.I.A. office, and when Klaus and I said we hoped to fly out of Chitral soon, he shook his head.

"There are three people waiting for every seat," he said. We nodded and told of our experience flying into Gilgit.

146

"Yes, it's the same here," he said. "The conditions are unreliable. One plane, a Fokker forty-seater, and we have a backlog of passengers. It may be three days or more before you can leave."

I was upset. I was due back within a week, and was anxious to get home a couple of days early to recuperate before going back to my office. The Shahzada noticed my expression, and said, gallantly, "Let me see what I can do." He picked up his gun and left the room, closing the door behind him. We sat in silence staring at each other. It was all so much like the Arabian Nights that we were speechless. Someone laughed softly, and then we all grinned.

"Ins' allah," I said. Things were so weird that I finally just quit worrying. This tough old man seemed to have taken us under his wing, and when he came back a few minutes later, it turned out that he would be able to get two seats. Waving his gun for emphasis, he stood in the middle of the room.

"The District Commissioner has two seats reserved for him on every flight. I have talked with him and he has consented to release his seats for tomorrow's flight."

Tom and Frank looked at each other, and nodded. Frank said, "This gentleman and I would like to take a two or three-day trip into Kaffiristan, so these other two can use the seats."

I felt my grin spread, and looking at Klaus nodded strenuously. The Shahzada looked pleased and it was arranged that late in the afternoon we would go to the D.C.'s office to complete the forms and procedures necessary to leave Chitral.

"In the meantime, I will invite you to my palace for lunch and to talk. I like very much to meet with foreigners; I have many friends all over the world."

We went back to our hotel to pull ourselves together, and an hour later, the Shahzada arrived with his jeep and driver. As we four climbed in awkwardly, a young boy of perhaps twelve scrambled up into the front seat to stand with the Shahzada and his shotgun. It turned out that he was the grandson and heir, since the Shahzada's son had died some years before. He had a proud attitude toward the boy, and put his arm protectively around him.

We drove a long way out of Chitral, back up into the moun-

147

tains, passing great barren fields with bands of sheep supervised by shepherds with dogs. Eventually we arrived at a series of large, low buildings, with a wide terrace in front of them. Huge trees shaded the terrace, flowers, and garden chairs. It was a strange combination of wild and tame, with this stocky, dark man stalking toward the house, gesturing with his gun for us to come along.

XXVII

The Shahzada ushered us into a reception room in the main building, then excused himself for a few minutes. While he was gone, we looked around at the walls, covered with photographs, swords, guns, game trophies. The room was long and narrow. A wide couch lined the entire length of each wall. Both were covered with pillows and soft rugs and they were separated by a low table that also ran the length of the room. We sat, two on each side of the table, feeling a bit lost among all the display. Everything was dusty, of course, but the sheer volume of knickknacks, lamps, memorabilia and weaponry was overwhelming.

After a moment, Frank got up and went to the end of the couch, where the Shahzada had carelessly thrown down his shotgun. Frank picked up the gun and stood it up in a corner of the room.

"It's probably loaded," he said, "and anyway, I nearly shot a friend of mine once when my loaded gun suddenly went off. He was just leaning over, or the bullet would have caught him. I'm pretty careful since then."

We all got up and began to inspect the room. The photographs covered earlier decades of the twentieth century, baby and childhood photos, school and RAF photos. The swords on the walls looked fierce and archaic, and the guns were of the blunderbuss variety. Massive animal heads and horns were elk, mountain goat, leopard. This room clearly bore the Shahzada's imprint.

He came back shortly, saying that he had ordered lunch, and would we drink something? We all nodded with enthusiasm. It was noon, now, and our stomachs were still clamorous for anything. To our mild disappointment we were offered orange and lemon squash, but anything was welcome at this point.

While we drank, our strange host talked. Apparently, his pleasure in visitors reflected a great need for an audience. He talked and talked, about his schooling in England, his tour with the RAF, the world visitors he had entertained. We signed a great book, and looked over the names in it. Indeed, people from all the continents had been here, most recently several groups of Japanese.

He told of the Japanese climbing expeditions, their successes and failures, also the Swiss and Germans. There had been few Americans through the area, and I felt as if we were now trophies for him. He described the political situation in the Pakistani Himalayas, the deep rift between the mountain provinces and the lowlands. He spoke eloquently of his dismay at the changing systems that were impinging on his four-hundred-year family history. It sounded as though his power was nearly drained away by the encroachment of Pakistan's government, and that his shotgun was a last ditch resource for stature. We asked him about his gun. He assured us that it was, indeed, loaded all the time. The danger of assassination was ever-present, he said, and he intended to take his assassin with him when the time came. It sounded so inevitable, his assassination, that I felt sad for him. Yet it may have been an unconscious acceptance of the end of the old order.

We listened to him talk, heard his need for our interest, and were touched. He was like a lion in captivity, uneasily domesticated, with the natural law of the wilderness humming just underneath. He spoke often of his dead son—we were too shy to ask how he died—and pointed out the window to the small hill on top of which the grave was centered. I felt that the Shahzada would not mind dying.

After an hour or so, lunch was brought in. trays and trays of meat, rice, potatoes, bread, tomatoes and soup. The servant who carried it all in was a dubious looking fellow, of whom the Shahzada said, between appearances, "He's not reliable. Too much drugs. Everywhere is too much drugs."

We realized then what the frenzied foreigners in the Chitral

PIA office may have been up to. Probably many of them were here for drugs. Judging from the bizarre appearance of some of them, they were consumers as well as dealers. The Shahzada seemed philosophical about it all, however, and while we ate, he began to define his attitudes about life. It was difficult at first to balance his statements of trust in the natural process, of yielding to the great forces of life, of participating energetically in the design of his days with the wild, fierce expression on his face, the tough gestures of his stocky body, the defiant set of his Hunza cap, which he wore throughout the meal.

The duality of this man was sharply delineated and I wondered at his capacity to preserve his psychic unity. He was at once the Prince and the subject, the Maker of Law and sufferer of its restriction. He was King and servant, past and present, primitive and civilized. That he had lived for sixty-five years under that stress was a tribute to his stamina. I wondered how much longer he would be able to sustain his existence.

At one point, he asked us a few questions, and Klaus and I talked a little about our family. He volunteered then that he had a wife, too, and she lived in one of the other buildings. Obviously the old customs prevailed and the women were secluded, for all this man's worldly experience with the West. He did not seem to notice any anomaly between his courtly attitude toward me and the exclusion of his wife from our gathering.

We ate everything, of course, only mildly discomfited by the fact that the servant's thumb had gone into most of the dishes. After all, he licked it off each time. As we finished, the Shahzada stood up suddenly and said, "I'd like you to taste my wine. I made it myself."

He produced two sticky bottles two-thirds full, one of light and the other of darker liquid. He poured us thimble-sized glasses of first one, and then the other. We drank it down stoically. It was viscous and bitter-sweet, really quite terrible, but it was clear that he was proud of it. Later, Klaus tried to arrange to have a case of California wine sent to him, but the red tape was too complex. Perhaps it is just as well that the Shahzada should not have had to know what we think wine really tastes like.

We were full of food now, and surfeited with this man's forceful nature and dammed up loneliness. I was tired beyond being able to listen any more, and wished I could disappear. Still he talked on. At long last, however, he indicated that he would take us to the District Commissioner's place to make arrangements for the next day's flight.

But first we had to troop out to the terrace, set up the garden chairs in a semi-circle, and take pictures. Only Frank had a camera, since we were uncomfortable about appearing too curious if we all brought our equipment. So, with Frank's camera, we photographed us all, in various combinations, with the Prince sitting proudly in the middle of each one. It was apparent that the modern man in him wanted recognition.

Then we all piled into the jeep again, the Shahzada clutching his gun by its throat as usual. We grinned anxiously at each other, and shrugged. The driver started off at a fine speed, and the palace was soon left behind in the dust.

152

XXVIII

The District Commissioner's office was on the other side of Chitral, up above the town on a shady knoll. It was a modern building surrounded by several others housing the D.C., his family, staff, and servants. The whole arrangement was intended apparently to inspire respect; as did the long wait we had until he consented to meet with us. For the hour or more that we had to sit there, we four and the Shahzada made desultory conversation. Periodically, a pale undernourished looking fellow would come in, nod at us, shuffle papers on the D.C.'s enormous desk, then leave again.

Since this was late afternoon, we assumed the District Commissioner was completing his afternoon nap. Indeed, when he finally appeared, he had the look of a man just arisen from sleep. A pudgy mollusk of a man, he eyed us with apparent distaste. We were, of course, a disreputable looking lot, with our torn and dirty clothing, our sunblackened faces and scraggly hair. Klaus's razor had failed after the first week of climbing and he had a white beard that made him look like the old man of the hills. The other two looked little better; Tom's beard was patchy, and though he was still shaving, Frank's loss of weight showed in his shrunken cheeks and baggy clothes.

The Shahzada introduced us, describing where we came from and what we had been doing. The D.C. seemed unable to see much to recommend us. It was lucky for us the Shahzada was able to perceive our sterling worth beneath our shabby exteriors. He spoke eloquently to the D.C. and we assumed he was pleading our case. It was an incredibly complicated business to acquire the two seats designated for the Commissioner's use, given that he did not even want them.

153

It was a problem of protocol, of course, and the power balance between the two men. Most of the conversation was carried on in Urdu. It seemed that the D.C. either would not, or could not, speak English. Apparently, he saw us as the Shahzada's conquests, and as such it may have suited him to treat us coolly. Certainly his manner with us lacked charm.

My heart sank as time went on and nothing seemed to be getting settled. The Shahzada sat in a big chair in front of the Commissioner's desk, while we four sat along the wall in a row beside the desk. Now and then, the thin young assistant would come in as before, fuss with something on the desk, exchange a few sentences with his boss and go out. The scene was becoming surreal, and in my fatigue, I began to think we would be refused seats after all.

After perhaps another hour during which nothing obvious happened apart from intermittent talk between the two men, the D.C. picked up the phone. He spoke briefly into it, hung up, pulled some papers out of a drawer, and looked at us without expression. The pale young man came in, was given the forms and our passports, and went away.

When we finally drove away in the Shahzada's jeep, Klaus and I had seats arranged for the early morning flight. We told the Shahzada of our appreciation for all his attention and effort, and in the garden of our hotel, took more pictures all around.

Dinner was the same menu as the night before, except that we ate by the light of a tiny candle. The electricity was out again, and candles were precious. We fell asleep right after dinner, and were up at five to catch the seven o'clock plane, but not until I had stuffed myself again with cornflakes.

The airstrip was a madhouse. Again the bizarre looking Europeans with their ployglot languages. Again the local gentry in pajama suits. And again the Shahzada with his double-barrelled shotgun held by the throat. He nodded at us, and took us to the official behind the desk in the cavernous shedlike building that was the airport's one facility.

After considerable pushing and shoving with the numerous people who apparently were hoping for cancellations, we got ourselves duly recorded and our luggage was hauled away. We watched it anxiously, as it was wheeled out to the edge of the landing strip.

Eventually the Fokker jet prop came in to land. We were loaded onto it along with our gear, and the little plane took off again. It was on the ground for not more than half an hour in all. It was most important to be on our way before the sun made the air too thin to sustain the plane.

The weather was also a threat. Heavy clouds were already beginning to form, and would soon make flying impossible, since navigation was dependent on visibility. As we rose from the airstrip, winds caught us and shook the small plane. The great mountains were all around us, so the captain took us up a narrow valley to gain altitude enough to clear the high ridges between the mountains. Chitral was seven or eight thousand feet, and the mountain peaks another five or ten thousand feet above that. The clouds were beginning to bunch up everywhere, and the flight was a terrifying experience.

Yet a steward brought us cardboard boxes of food, and tea in paper cups. He seemed comfortable enough in these difficult circumstances, with the plane bouncing and shaking wildly. So we dared to watch the passing scenery even though it was horrifying. We skimmed over ridges so closely we could see individual rocks. Great peaks rose above us on all sides; the little plane flew around and between them.

After about an hour of flying among the mountains, we could see the lower plains of Pakistan appear. Soon we began to fly over descending ridges and there were no more mountains higher than we were. Gradually we approached the plains, and finally the mountains fell behind us.

It was to my great surprise that I felt regret to be leaving the Himalayas. How perverse of me, I thought, here I am, getting what I have wanted for weeks, and instead of feeling glad, I am sorry. I suppose "nostalgic" might be a better word. Certainly if anyone had offered to fly me back into the mountains I would have declined unhesitatingly. Nonetheless, it had been an extraordinary time for me, and I

155

still face the difficult task of processing the whole thing. I am only now, this much later, beginning to feel that I know something of what happened to me in that vast, strange country. Writing this account has been an important part of that process.

We landed safely in Peshawar, were delayed by rains for a few hours, then flew the brief distance to Rawalpindi. There we stayed for a few days trying to get a flight to Karachi, a thousand miles to the south. The monsoons still had everything in confusion, and flying was the only means of transportation available. We did finally find a Pakistani travel agent willing to push for seats for us on a PIA flight. Most airline ticket agents preferred to let Allah provide seats, so we were delighted by this fellow's energy. He booked us on a connecting flight at Karachi for Athens and Zurich. We started eating on the Karachi flight, continued to eat on the Swiss Air flight, and arrived in Zurich sick as can be. Our systems had learned to manage on tea and peanuts, and were appalled by the richness of the food we were eating on the planes. We had a six-hour wait in Zurich's airport and spent the time lying flat on the benches or trooping to the bathroom. We flew from Zurich to New York, waited a couple more hours, then flew the last leg to San Francisco. It was a fifteen thousand mile trip home from Rawalpindi, Pakistan, and it took us thirty-six hours of flying and airport waiting time. As we drove up to our house in San Francisco, we looked at each other blankly. The disorientation of being in civilization again was disturbing enough, but far more disturbing was the feeling of being stuffed with an experience so raw, so jagged and out of this world that we could choke on it.

It was several months before we could speak of the trip at all without getting caught in a torrent of description uncontrollably welling up from our depths. It was four months before I dared to begin to write out my impressions; until then the power of the experience was too great. As I concluded the first draft, nine months had passed. Perhaps the analogy to gestation is appropriate.

AFTERWORD

One might reasonably ask why Klaus and I, middle-aged and inexperienced, undertook this trip into the Hindu Kush. Our expressed reasons at the time were insufficient. We have come to realize that.

It is now exactly three years later, and I know more about what moved us to join the expedition.

Then, we thought we were going on a regular, if strenuous trek, over terrain familiar to our guides. Now, we recognize that we did have enough information, before we went, to alert us to the exploratory nature of the trip. Perhaps we would not have gone had we allowed this knowledge to surface to consciousness.

Then, we thought we wanted to enjoy, close up, the glorious mountain fortress we had seen from a great distance in Alma-Ata, near Tashkent in Russian Central Asia. Now, we realize that we wanted to immerse ourselves in those great mountains, mold into them, discover their center.

Then, we thought this was our last chance to undertake a strenuous adventure before we were too old. Now (and here I speak only for myself), I realize that I was at a mid-life crisis, and was seeking enlightenment about my ambivalence toward life.

It is this last issue that has preoccupied me since returning from the Himalayas. It took one year to write the story and two more to get it ready for publication. During the three years I have thought long about the question of how, and even, if, to live out the rest of my life.

While in the Himalayas I had the repeated experience of being helped by previously unrealized reserves of strength, when I thought I was finished. Klaus and I had, over and over again, extraordinary good luck in getting through terrible situations that could so easily have resulted in death for either or both of us.

That I survived the trip is beyond my understanding. That Klaus was delivered out of that monsoon-bedeviled rockfall is unexplainable. He, himself, cannot really comprehend his coming through safely.

I feel that I have been given the balance of my life. I find now that I can accept the gift.

I learned this in the Himalayas, and in some unexplained way, I knew that I would if I dared to go there. But I would never have dared had it not been that Klaus dared, too. This was truly a shared ordeal.